SOLSTICE MOON

THE UPHEAVAL BOOK 3

CHARLEY MARSH

TIMBERDOODLE PRESS

1

JORDAN JAMES SLOWLY, reluctantly, awoke, aware that something was amiss. Dogma was no longer beside him. He heard her growl low in her chest and realized her growl had wakened him. Wide awake now, he automatically reached for his staff but it was gone.

He stilled, using the senses that had sharpened since he lost his sight, to test his surroundings. He heard birdsong, a slight breeze high in the treetops, and Dogma's warning growl. He opened his eyes and gasped with surprise.

Four auras were bent over him, their pulsating fields of energy meeting over his body in a strange canopy of colored light.

The ability to see auras was a recent development for Jordan. He could not only discern people and animals, but plants and rocks as well, a fact he had only shared with his friend and traveling companion, Sydney Waters.

"Who are you?" he asked the figures bent over him, striving to hide his fear under a stern voice. The auras didn't answer. He slowly sat up, resisting the urge to clutch his blanket to his bare chest as a shield from their prying eyes. The auras straightened, giving him room to sit upright, but didn't step back.

"I said, who are you?" he demanded again, louder and sterner. Still no answer. Now that he was sitting he could see two more auras standing off to the side. Six against one. Terrible odds, even with Dogma. He couldn't take the chance that they were armed, wouldn't risk Dogma's life that way. If he could see and was armed himself maybe he could fight them.

If only, if only. He had learned early on in his life not to dwell on if-onlys. They only depressed him. If only his parents hadn't come to his baseball game. If only the drunk who hit their car had passed out before getting behind the wheel. If only someone had taken the drunk's keys away so he couldn't drive.

After a while a person had to stop looking behind and concentrate on looking forward instead. Otherwise they'd grow bitter and hard.

Jordan's blanket was snatched away from him. Too late, he tried to hang on to it. Dogma's growl grew louder but the auras seemed unbothered by the large dog. Who were they? Two pairs of hands grabbed each upper arm and hauled him to his feet. One of the auras bent down and then he felt his second blanket draped over his bare shoulders. They gathered around him, two on each side with the fifth in front and the last following, boxing him in.

Dogma pushed through the bodies and pressed against his thigh. He wound his fingers tight in her thick ruff and concentrated on keeping his expression blank.

"Where are you taking me?" Still no answer. His escorts were a band of mutes. Wouldn't that be ironic, he mused. Me blind, them dumb. Or perhaps they're a band of monks who have taken the vow of silence and they're escorting me to their monastery. Perhaps they want to recruit me.

It was possible. They had found him alone in the forest, perhaps they thought they were rescuing him. They had no way of knowing he wasn't traveling alone. He didn't dare tell them about Sydney. If they turned out to be bad people he didn't want to put her in danger. If they knew she was out there somewhere nearby they would look for her, he felt sure of it.

He didn't want to think about how Sydney would feel when she returned from hunting and found him gone. She would panic, thinking he had somehow wandered off and become lost. He tried to think of a way to leave her a message but nothing came to mind.

"Where is my staff? he demanded in a loud voice. "I'm blind, I need my staff."

The group stopped. No one spoke, then his staff was pushed into his hand and they began to walk again.

The return of his staff eased some of Jordan's tension. His captors, whoever they were, couldn't mean him ill if they were willing to let him keep Dogma and his only weapon. For a brief moment he considered lashing out at them. He could easily take down half the group if he caught them by surprise. His hands tightened on his staff, then relaxed. No, it was better to go with them peacefully and see what they wanted with him. With no hospitals or medicine it was dangerous and foolhardy to risk a serious injury.

He wished his captors would speak, if not to him then at least to each other. Their continued silence was eerie and unsettling.

Jordan took a deep breath, sucking in the sweet smell of

dead pine needles and the sharp pungent odor of evergreen, odors he had never smelled before yesterday. He had been born and raised in Iowa and traveled the world performing on the piano before the earth's great upheaval. Whisked from plane to limo to hotel to concert hall and back home again, he had never ventured beyond his family farm or a city's limits before meeting Sydney.

He felt the play of light and shadow upon his face and shoulders. The trail--*he assumed they were on some sort of trail*--climbed and dipped. He concentrated on putting one foot in front of the other and regulated his breathing, glad that he was in better physical condition than he'd ever been. All the miles that he and Sydney had walked together had done him good.

He grew confused despite his efforts to keep track of the direction his captors were leading him. The trail twisted and turned until a general ascension was the only thing he felt sure of. The trail steepened and he was glad of the staff. He wondered how long they had been walking. He wondered where they were leading him. He wondered if Sydney would be able to follow or if he had seen the last of her. The thought of not being with Sydney again made him feel sick to his stomach.

They hiked until he felt the last of the sun's rays on his left cheek, telling him they had turned north. The group stopped and silently set up camp. They gave Jordan his sleeping gear and set their own bedding around him, making it impossible to escape without stepping on one of them. They broke camp with the first cold light of dawn and handed Jordan a piece of jerky to eat as they walked.

After half a day's travel the trail leveled off and Jordan realized they were walking through an alpine meadow. He heard the faint buzz of bees and other insects collecting pollen and smelled the fresh sweetness of some flower he couldn't identify. The sound of flowing water reached his ears. A mountain stream, he realized.

The air held a brisk edge to it and he pulled the blanket tighter around his bare shoulders. His request for his shirt had been ignored. He wondered if his captors had brought along his bag. He was going to need warmer clothes if they intended to keep him here for any length of time.

The thought made him lose his concentration and he stumbled and jerked forward. Hands grabbed both arms and held him upright, then released him. The group never slowed. They were like automatons, silent and unstoppable.

It was at that moment that Jordan realized his life had changed once more. Unless Sydney managed to track and find him he was doomed to remain with the silent ones forever, or as long as forever turned out to be. Escape was out of the question. A blind man alone in the mountains? There was no way he could survive, even with his second sight. If he was lucky he'd fall off a cliff and die immediately, otherwise he'd wander, lost forever, and slowly starve to death.

The thought frustrated and depressed the hell out of him.

Several minutes later the lead aura began to rise. At the same time Jordan heard boots on wood. Steps! He looked up and sensed a large building looming over the group. Hands grasped his arms again and guided him up the stairs. The sun on his back disappeared and they walked across what he took to be a covered porch.

The group stopped. A heavy metal knocker sounded three times. They waited what was probably only several minutes but it felt like an eternity to Jordan. Where were they? What happens now? He had a feeling that he was about to discover if his captors were friendly or if he was about to be brought before an evil leader and sacrificed at the evening ceremonies.

He scratched between Dogma's ears and tried to appear nonchalant while they waited. She seemed reasonably calm and he took heart from that. Perhaps he had been found by a local clan of do-gooders and would be fed and housed for the rest of his days.

The door squeaked open. He heard the low murmur of a woman's voice, then hands guided him over the door stoop and into the building. Jordan had the sensation of standing in a large hall, but he couldn't be sure. His six escorts still surrounded him and Dogma while a seventh aura walked away from them and abruptly disappeared.

Again they waited, this time for a much longer spell. Jordan started to fidget.

"Do you guys have any food? I've missed a number of meals and I'm pretty hungry." He spun around in shock when a woman's voice answered from behind him.

"Don't worry, you will be fed soon enough. What is your name?"

Her voice sounded stern and uncompromising and he had the impression of a school teacher or governess. Someone who expected to be obeyed and have her questions answered or else.

Or else what?

"I am Jordan James, at your service, ma'am," he said. It never hurt to be polite. "Who are you and where are we?"

"My name is unimportant. Where you are is unimportant. Were you traveling alone?"

"Yes." Jordan was glad he hadn't mentioned Sydney. Something about the situation and the woman questioning him made him feel uneasy. Even though no one had threatened him–*yet*–he sensed that something was amiss.

"Mallory Dunne will see you in good time and will decide what to do about you. Wait here until your presence is requested." His interrogator turned and exited the hall through a different door than the one the seventh aura had used. Three of his escorts broke off and trailed behind her.

Well, one of them can speak at least. What do you make of this situation, Mr. Piano Man? Apparently he was not in a monastery, or they were an equal opportunity organization and allowed women to join their ranks. Something told him his captors were not monks.

He wondered who Mallory Dunne was. And how large the building they were in was. He sensed a great deal of bulk around him and guessed that the building was substantial, if only from the way the entry hall echoed.

He ran his hands over the ram's head carving on top of his staff and wondered where Sydney was and what she thought of his disappearance. Would she be able to track him through the pine forest or would the thick bed of needles that carpeted the forest floor hide all traces of his passage?

He had no idea. He had become blind too early in his life to learn the skill of tracking. Not that anyone would've taught him. He had assumed he would follow in his father's footsteps and become a farmer. Raise corn and soybeans. After the accident that took his parent's lives and his sight his sister helped him focus on music so he could support himself.

But Sydney was a capable young woman who knew her way around the wilderness and he had faith in her. If anyone could find him he would place his bet on her. The problem was he didn't know yet if he wanted her to find him. He didn't know how dangerous this Mallory Dunne, whoever he or she was, would turn out to be.

Jordan frowned. He didn't want to expose Sydney to any more danger. It seemed that everywhere they went they ran into some nutcase and ended up fighting for their lives. First Driftwood and the gang of escaped convicts, then Graceville with its crazy citizens. Now…now what? he wondered.

2

SYDNEY SUCKED THE CLEAN, crisp air deep into her lungs. She reveled in the sharp smell of pine and balsam and the deep evergreen color that covered the mountainside. The foothills of the Rocky mountains were a welcome change after the bleak, colorless desert that used to be Nebraska farm country.

It had taken two weeks of steady travel, first in the Gator their friend Silas had gifted them, and then on foot when they ran out of gas, to reach water, forests, and a source of food again. She and Jordan had endured a long week of terrible heat and eventually thirst. Near the end she had despaired that they would survive.

But survive they did. Even the two russet-colored hens, Henrietta and Ginny, had endured. They were now happily chasing insects and pulling fresh green shoots back at camp.

Sydney smiled. She had left her two companions stretched out side by side, sleeping on a deep, soft pile of pine needles while she hunted for fresh squirrel meat for the soup pot. Jordan James, a handsome, blind piano player and his giant dog had proven themselves to be entertaining and loyal friends. She felt fortunate to have their companionship.

When she set out from her family farm on the banks of the Mississippi River several months ago she had had no idea how difficult and dangerous the trek across the country would be, especially for a young woman alone. Hooking up with Jordan and Dogma had turned out to be a blessing in disguise.

She popped out of the forest onto a rock promontory. Pale gray-green lichen covered the granite surface in delicate whorls shaped like the petals of a prehistoric flower. She stepped carefully so her heavy hiking boots wouldn't damage it. She knew that lichen took years, many, many years, to establish itself.

Although Sydney had always respected the natural world, she had become even more conscious of man's effect upon the wilderness after the upheaval, when Mother Nature had said "Enough," and risen up against mankind to take back her planet.

Sydney looked out over the wilderness stretching before her. The view from her perch was spectacular. Rolling green foothills were backed by tall mountain peaks that piled up one after the other, disappearing into the silvery mist as far as she could see. Snow dripped over the uppermost reaches like icing on her favorite angel food cake.

She sighed with a sharp, piercing longing. Her mother had always made two cakes for her birthday: angel food for Sydney and chocolate with chocolate frosting topped with coconut for her twin Shannon. Shannon was crazy about coconut. She used to eat it straight from its bag.

Now they were both gone, her mother taken by the tsunamis that hit the east coast, and her sister raped and murdered by the Desperate Ones who roamed the countryside after the disaster. Sydney had tasted her last birthday cake a lifetime ago.

The pain of her loss was still sharp and immediate, but it didn't send her into the emotional downward spiral that usually caught her when she thought of her family.

Perhaps she was starting to heal, to become reconciled with her losses. Mother, father, sister, grandfather--all gone, leaving her alone to face a dangerous new world.

Sydney thought about that as she watched a bald eagle soar on the updrafts flowing along the foothills, looking for food, just as she was. Was she starting to forget the people dearest to her?

No. She would never forget her family, never forget the beast who had taken her sister, her better half, from her. Nor would she ever forget how her cowardice had prevented her from going to her sister's aid. She knew intellectually that she would have met the same fate as Shannon if she had, but her heart still condemned her for her lack of courage.

Sydney turned and plunged back into the forest. Survival meant focusing on the now. Dwelling on the past didn't put food in their bellies. She heard the rapid chatter of an aggravated red squirrel and went to look for him, nocking an arrow in her bow as she went. She would think of Shannon later. Right now she had two hungry companions waiting for her back at their campsite.

Two hours later Sydney walked into camp holding three squirrels aloft.

"I found dinner! We won't go to bed hungry tonight."

No reply. Puzzled, she lowered the squirrels and looked around the deserted camp. She spotted Henrietta and Ginny tied to their downed limb off to the edge of the small clearing, scratching in the ground cover and clucking softly.

"Jordan? Dogma!" Sydney raised her voice and hollered

for The Great Beast, her affectionate nickname for Jordan's canine guide and protector. Perhaps Jordan had woken and wanted to stretch his legs and explore. It was the only explanation she could find for the deserted camp.

Even though he had been blinded as a young boy in an auto accident, since hooking up with Sydney, Jordan James had developed extraordinary skills that allowed him to function with relative ease in his dark world. His uncanny ability to sense objects had grown to the point where he rarely bumped into anything anymore.

More recently he had acquired the ability to see the auras of animals, plants, and people. Jordan rarely behaved like a man with a handicap and Sydney often forgot that he was blind.

Only he was.

Sydney frowned. What if he had wandered off and fallen? He could have walked onto a rocky point like the one Sydney had found earlier and walked right off the edge. He could be lying in a ravine with a broken leg, unconscious, even bleeding to death…or mauled and carried off by a bear or mountain lion.

Panic rose in her chest. "JORDAN!" Sydney called as loud as she could, turned in the opposite direction and called again. She listened, hands cupped to her ears to magnify sound. She heard nothing but the soft whisper of a gentle breeze wafting through the pine and fir treetops.

It was then she realized that the bed of pine needles where she had left Jordan sleeping peacefully was empty, Jordan's blankets gone. She looked around the campsite and saw that his pack was missing as well.

Surely a wild animal would not have taken Jordan's possessions. Either Jordan took them himself for some reason she didn't understand, or they had been stolen.

"Oh no." Sydney ran to the log next to the hens and heaved a sigh of relief. Her pack lay where she had placed it, behind the log where it would be out of Jordan's way. She stood and turned a complete circle. *Where was he?* It wasn't like him to take off without letting her know. If he needed to be by himself for a while he simply told her he needed alone time and she obliged, no big deal.

Something was very, very wrong. Even if Jordan had felt like taking a walk after his nap he would not have taken his pack and blankets with him. They had agreed to stop traveling for a few days, to remain in this spot while they recovered from the ordeal of crossing the Nebraskan desert.

Where was he????

The sun dipped below the mountains and the air temperature immediately dropped to near freezing. Sydney built a small, smokeless fire using the dead branches she had gathered that morning. She cleaned her squirrels and placed them in a pot with some water from a nearby spring.

Despite her efforts to act as if nothing was wrong, unease made her nervous. Jordan should have returned by now. Dogma would've led him back to their campsite, she felt sure of it. Where could he have gone? Even if he had felt the need to be by himself for a while he wouldn't have taken his duffle bag. Jordan's disappearance made no sense.

She stood and walked to the edge of the small clearing and peered into the gathering gloom. She had looked for Jordan's tracks earlier but found nothing to indicate which direction he had taken. This was so unlike him. He would never knowingly make her worry like this.

Frustrated, she walked to the opposite edge of the clearing and peered through the trees, hoping to see Jordan and Dogma making their way back to her. She saw nothing but dark trunks fading into deep shadow. "Damn you, Jordan," she whispered.

She returned to her fire and sat on the ground, leaning back against the large boulder that had caught her eye several days earlier, the reason she had chosen this site to make camp. She made an effort to push any thoughts of Jordan lying somewhere injured from her mind. Thinking negative thoughts never helped any situation. She knew that, but it was still an easy trap to fall into.

She reminded herself of the story her friend and mentor Smokey had once told her about an old man who carried a trunk containing all his worldly possessions aboard a train. Once on the train he refused to set the trunk down and let the train carry the burden, even though the trunk was very heavy and hurt his back.

"Don't be like that foolish old man, Sydney," Smokey had told her. "Let the Great Spirit who abides in every living thing carry your burdens. Trust that it will take care of you."

It was a lesson she constantly struggled with.

The squirrels finished cooking and Sydney forced herself to eat one even though worry had robbed her appetite. She looked at the two remaining squirrels, one for Jordan and one for Dogma, and tears filled her eyes. She dashed them away with the back of her sleeve.

Tomorrow she would begin the search for her companions. She could do nothing in the dark except wait for dawn's light. Sydney hung the leftover meat in a tree away from the clearing in case a bear or mountain lion came hunting, then shook out her sleeping bag and laid it next to the boulder. She carefully put out the campfire with the extra water she had carried for that purpose, and crawled into her bag.

Images of Jordan and Dogma lying broken at the bottom of a steep mountain ravine flashed in her mind's eye. She firmly pushed them away. "I will not dwell on the negative," she told herself firmly. "They are safe and sound, only lost and waiting for me to find them." Sydney closed her eyes and willed sleep to come. Fortunately the hot meal combined with utter exhaustion soon dragged her into a fitful sleep.

JORDAN'S LEGS WERE TIRED. He wanted to sit. He wanted to eat. He wanted to put a shirt on and cover his naked chest. He was tired of standing around the entryway, tired of waiting with the silent auras. He grasped the blanket more firmly, giving in to the need to hide himself from any curious eyes.

"Is this going to take long?" he asked, "because I have places to go and I really need to be on my way."

The three auras ignored him. Just when Jordan thought he couldn't continue to stand one moment longer, his interrogator returned.

"Mallory will see you now. Follow me."

Hands urged Jordan after her receding aura. They reached a wall and turned right. He felt carpet under his feet, sensed walls on both sides and a long space before him. I'm in a hallway, he realized.

His escorts hustled him down the hall and stopped at what felt like the midpoint. They turned him a quarter turn until he faced a wall. Now what?

Jordan heard the muffled murmur of many female voices.

He strained to hear the deeper tone of men but heard none. Was this a women's meeting? Why were they bringing him to a women's meeting? A small shiver of fear raced down his back. Was he on the program as today's sacrifice?

He didn't know what brought the image of a sacrificial alter to his mind but he wished he hadn't thought of it. Recent experience had taught him that with the world gone crazy human sacrifice was a real possibility.

The interrogator pulled open the door and Jordan forced himself to stand straighter and shake off his fear. Whatever he was about to face he resolved to face with dignity.

The voices grew louder and then suddenly stopped. His captors escorted him through the door and he found himself in a large room filled with auras. The auras parted into two groups and Jordan was led between them to the front of the room.

Like the parting of the Red Sea, only he wasn't Moses.

Jordan picked up the faint smell of sweet perfume and burning sage. *At least this group keeps themselves clean.* They stopped in front of three auras standing above shoulder height.

Unless these three are floating in the air they're standing on some kind of dais or a stage. One of these must be the mysterious Mallory Dunne. He bowed his head briefly toward the three and waited for someone to speak. The room remained silent although he could hear the others breathing and feel their collected body heat.

Nothing happened for several long minutes. Jordan had the sense he was being inspected. Anger began to replace his fear. Who did these women think they were, treating a stranger so rudely? He thrust his chin forward and took a breath to speak.

"Jordan James, what brings you to our mountain?"

The voice was lovely: smooth and melodic, mesmerizing. Jordan immediately forgave her for keeping him waiting. Any woman who possessed a voice this beautiful had to be a lovely person.

"I am a simple traveler, ma'am. Dogma and I are searching for a place to call home. We wandered here after crossing the Nebraska desert." Best to stick as close to the truth as possible.

"You crossed the desert? No one has attempted that and survived." The voice held a hint of sharpness and surprise now. If Jordan's hearing were not so acute he would have missed it. Apparently Mallory Dunne didn't like the thought of someone crossing the desert. He wondered why that bothered her.

"It was a near thing," he answered. "We barely made it to the foothills and water." If it hadn't been for Sydney he and Dogma would be long dead. She was the one who unerringly led them to a small stream on the desert's edge.

Jordan decided it was his turn to ask questions. "Who are you and what is this place?"

"I am Mallory Dunne, High Priestess of the Temple of Gaia."

Jordan frowned. "Isn't Gaia another name for earth? I'm sure I've heard that word somewhere before. Is it Hindu or Indian possibly?"

"Very good, Master James." Mallory gave a low chuckle. "It is indeed the word for earth, but it is from Greek mythology, not the Far East. Gaia was a goddess, the daughter of Chaos, mother and wife of Heaven. She is earth personified and has recently made her presence known to lowly men."

Jordan chose to ignore the comment about lowly men. For now. "Hmmm, it sounds a little kinky to be the mother *and* the wife of someone, wouldn't you agree? A little inces-tuous perhaps?"

"Not when we are discussing the Gods, Master James. They are not governed by the petty rules and hangups of man." The sharpness in her tone was more pronounced now. It gave Jordan a small jolt of satisfaction to learn that he could get a rise out of the High Priestess.

"My apologies, Ms. Dunne. My comment was in poor taste. Perhaps you could tell me where this temple is located. I'm sure it is lovely, but as you know, I am blind and am unable to fully appreciate what I'm sure is a beautiful place."

"Apology accepted, Master James. Our temple is indeed lovely. It was once a private retreat owned by a multi-billion dollar corporation. We sit on the side of a mountain with panoramic views and a mountain stream complete with waterfall and alpine meadows. It is a place that has been blessed by Gaia." A murmur of amens sounded behind Jordan.

"Is there anything you would like to tell us about yourself, Master James? We can see that you are a very handsome man, indeed, other than your blindness you are a fine spec-imen of the male of our species."

Jordan felt the heat rise in his neck and cheeks. He had never gotten used to hearing himself labeled as handsome and he wasn't sure he liked being referred to as a specimen. "Thank you," he muttered.

"Have you been blind from birth?" Although the question was asked in a friendly manner Jordan got the distinct impression that the answer was important for some reason.

"No, I was born sighted. I lost my vision in a car accident as a young boy."

"Very good. I am sorry about the accident of course, but

happy to hear that your affliction is not congenital. Is there anything else you care to share with us?"

Jordan wondered why the timing of his blindness mattered. "Hmm, well, I play piano fairly well and can sing. Before the upheaval I performed around the world and entertained royalty."

"What you refer to as the upheaval was a long overdue reckoning, Master James. We of the Temple of Gaia celebrate it as the new beginning. The Goddess Gaia has asserted herself and taken back control of her planet from the greedy who were destroying it. Those of us who recognize Gaia and honor and worship her will survive and prosper."

"I beg to differ, Ms. Dunne. Many good people lost their lives in the catastrophe that shook our planet. Many not-so-good ones as well, I admit, but what of the innocents who died?"

"No one is truly innocent, Master James. We all carry the sins of our pasts with us. History has always recorded the deaths of innocents, collateral damage cannot be avoided. Those souls will be blessed in their next reincarnation. It is none of our concern."

Jordan thought back to the town of Driftwood and the young children who had suffered as pawns of the criminal Pharaoh. "I have to disagree with you I'm afraid. I believe we have a responsibility to do all we can to protect the innocent."

"Believe what you will, Master James. I think we've talked enough. You will be taken to your room while I confer with my followers and then we will dine. Lorelei, will you please escort Master James to his quarters and find him a robe to wear?"

Jordan recognized the interrogator's voice as she bid him follow her from the meeting room. "So your name is Lorelei?

Pretty name. Can you tell me how many people live in the Temple of Gaia?"

Lorelei said nothing for several minutes. Just when Jordan thought she wasn't going to answer, she spoke.

"There are fifty of us. Mallory is very selective about who may join us. Only fifty of the healthiest and well built women are invited to live in Gaia's Temple." There was a hint of pride in her voice.

Fifty women? And why only the healthy and well-built ones? Was this the Temple of Lesbos? What the hell was going on here?

"The hotel must be very large," said Jordan aloud. He struggled to keep his tone neutral. "That's a lot of people to house and feed. How do you manage it?"

"Mallory has the acolytes split into groups. There are cooks, gardeners, housekeepers, seamstresses, weavers, laundresses, and animal tenders. We are set up the way a lord would have run a feudal castle. There is also an outside group of men who cut and stack firewood for us and perform other chores that require a man's superior strength."

Jordan stopped short. He watched Lorelei's aura walk ahead, then return to him. "Are you telling me men are not allowed to live in the temple?" he asked.

"Of course not. This is the Temple of Gaia after all. Only women are allowed to live here, therefore women must perform all the necessary duties." She pulled at his shirt sleeve to get him walking again, then pressed lightly on Jordan's arm and turned him down a corridor.

"Then where are all the men living? Shouldn't I be bunking with them?" He was feeling less comfortable with the situation by the minute. What did these women want with him?

Now that he had time to consider the circumstances, he

didn't understand why they had brought him here instead of leaving him in the forest. Surely he had no value. A blind man cannot gather or split firewood.

"The men? Why they live in the woodcutter's cottage of course." She then verified Jordan's thoughts. "Obviously you are of no use to us as a woodcutter, therefore it is inappropriate for you to bunk with them. You will stay here until Mallory determines where you should go." She placed her hand on Jordan's arm again and stopped him.

Jordan heard a door open next to them. "Then why am I here?" he asked. "I don't understand."

Lorelei guided him into his room and then stepped back into the hall. "The High Priestess and her assistants are considering your usefulness to us. They will inform you when they have decided."

Jordan whirled around and stepped toward the door. "Wait! What happens to the men you have no use for?"

He heard the door close. He stumbled forward and felt for the knob but found he had been locked in. He had a feeling he wasn't going to like the answer to what Ms. Dunne's group did with the men. Apparently these followers of Gaia only value the female of the species.

"Dogma? Are you here?" He searched the empty room for Dogma's aura. They had taken his great beast from him. No Dogma and no Sydney. A deep loneliness washed over him. He dropped to the thick carpet and stretched out by the door, waiting for someone to come and tell him why he was there if no men were allowed in the temple.

After the last of the acolytes had filed from the meeting room Mallory turned to her two personal aides. "He'll do," she said with satisfaction. "He's a fine specimen. We're fortunate our seekers found him. Make sure he is fed well and gets everything he needs."

4

SYDNEY LAY on top of her sleeping bag and watched the sunlight filter through the tree branches overhead. Small brown birds, impossible to identify because they were back-lit, flitted among the branches. Occasionally a yellowed leaf detached itself and fluttered slowly to the ground.

Soon the snows would arrive. She could already smell it in the air.

It was time for a new plan of action. She had waited an entire day in the campsite clearing for Jordan and Dogma to return. That evening she realized they were not coming back. That meant one of two things; either Jordan was hurt or lost, or he had decided to leave her and strike out on his own.

After much consideration she dismissed the second possibility. Her heart told her that Jordan cared too much for her to simply leave without talking to her first. Therefore he must be lying hurt somewhere.

She spent the next four days searching for him. Each day, using the sun to guide her, she started from their campsite and headed off in a different direction. She scrambled down into every ravine, searched every pile of boulders and behind downed trees, shouted until she grew hoarse and eventually lost her voice.

She stumbled back to the campsite at near dark, legs so tired she could barely lift her feet and place them one in front of another. She felt weary to the bone and heartsick. She could find no sign of her friend.

It was time to accept that Jordan had left her without an explanation or a goodbye. The truth cut into her like an icy, dull blade and shattered her heart into tiny, sharp pieces. It was hard to accept that she'd meant so little to him. She had assumed they were going to build a life together.

Instead she found herself alone in the world—again. Only this time it felt much, much worse.

She heard the hens cluck excitedly. Now that they were finding insects and greens to eat they were laying eggs again, a boon for Sydney. She could survive for a short while on eggs and edible greens, at least until she felt inspired to hunt again.

She forced herself to her feet and wandered over to gather the hen's two offerings. At least the hens were company of sorts. Ginny and Henrietta had grown quite tame and even allowed her to hold them in her lap and stroke their soft feathered backs, much like pet cats.

Sydney considered her situation while she waited for this morning's eggs to boil.

It was time to put Jordan James behind her and resume her original journey.

Time to find her friend Smokey and establish a new life before she became trapped in the mountains by the heavy snows.

Time to build a life without Jordan, the man she'd grown to love.

She pressed her lips together and choked back a sob. She would not let Jordan's abandonment get to her. She had obviously misunderstood his affectionate words and kisses. She had been sucked in by his handsome face and charm and her desperate need to feel close to someone. She wouldn't let that ever happen again.

Apparently Jordan's new ability to sense objects and see the auras of living things had given him the courage to go his own way. He no longer needed her. She wouldn't think about how he would feed himself. Wouldn't think about what he would do if he encountered a bear or a wolf or a mountain lion. He had Dogma to protect him.

She had survived the loss of her family and she would survive this loss as well.

Sydney forced down the hot eggs and broke camp, relegating her pain into the same space that housed the memories of her grandfather and the day she had watched her twin sister raped and murdered.

She gathered the hens and placed them in their cages, donned her pack and found herself a stout walking stick. The stick reminded her of the staff she had carved for her grandfather from an old ironwood tree that once stood near her grandfather's barn. She had been particularly proud of the ram's head with its curling horns, a symbol of her grandfather's reputation as a breeder of prize-winning sheep.

Jordan carried that staff now. Sydney hoped it would remind him of her in the years ahead; remind him of the friend he had abandoned without even a goodbye.

Sydney turned north, picking up and following animal trails wherever possible. Animals knew how to traverse the rugged landscape. They stayed off the ridges where they were exposed to the wind and the eyes of predators.

She kept her crossbow pistol loaded and handy with extra

bolts in the quiver that hung like a gunslinger's holster on her left hip. The bolts were too small to stop a bear, but they might convince one she wasn't worth pursuing.

She emptied her mind and focused on the beauty around her, letting Mother Nature work her magic on her wounded soul. There was peace to be found in the wilderness, the kind of peace that only came when all else was stripped away, leaving only a woman's connection to the essence and continuation of life.

5

JORDAN WOKE up on his second day in the temple and discovered his clothes had been taken and a thick, rough robe left in its place. The sleeves were slightly too short and it barely reached his calves, but he preferred it to walking around naked.

He wondered how they had managed to take his clothing without waking him. Had they put something in his food to drug him? And where was Dogma? He needed the great beast.

Lorelei, his appointed guide and watchdog, led him to the dining room for breakfast. The dining room was large, filled with round tables, the sound of clinking china and flatware, and the low hum of female conversation. Jordan knew the tables were round because he saw the auras arranged in circular shapes.

He wished he could see their faces and talk with them, but it had been made clear at the beginning of his stay that he was not to speak to the acolytes. Only Lorelei or Mallory Dunne were allowed to converse with him.

Jordan's acute hearing picked up low whispers as Lorelei led him in a winding path through the curious women to an empty table near one edge of the room.

"That's Jordan James. Lorelei says he might be the one." Soft giggles and murmurs too low to make out followed.

The one what? wondered Jordan. But in spite of repeated efforts to get information from Lorelei he learned nothing.

The food was good and plentiful and he ate his fill at each meal that followed. There seemed to be plenty of fresh meat, vegetables, and even bread, something he hadn't tasted in several years.

His tastebuds reveled in the first blissful bite of a warm biscuit topped with soft butter and berry jam and he moaned with the pleasure of it. Several auras nearby giggled and were sharply admonished.

He felt a bit like a bug being examined under a microscope, his every move watched and remarked upon. The biscuit turned to a lump of paste in his mouth and he struggled to swallow it.

His life had fallen into a strictly structured routine. Breakfast, time outside to get fresh air–usually a guided walk around the meadow or to the waterfall–lunch, then a nap followed by piano time. (The retreat boasted a beautiful grand piano.)

He attended guided meditation with the acolytes in the late afternoons followed by bath, dinner, and finally bed.

His daily requests for Dogma's return were ignored, although his cleaned clothes had been returned to him when he refused to walk about in a short robe.

The only time he was alone was when he was locked inside his room for a nap or bath and during the night. Despite his continued efforts to speak with the other girls, only Lorelei spoke to him. Lorelei kept her conversation limited to short sentences, never speaking unless spoken to and she often ignored his questions.

He missed his discussions with Sydney. Although she lacked the worldly travels and exposure that Jordan had enjoyed, Sydney had proved to be a well-read and interesting person with strong opinions and a willingness to share and to question and learn. She also possessed a quirky sense of humor that made him laugh. With Sydney he could engage in a heated disagreement without fear of hurting their friendship.

God, he missed her.

He wondered where Sydney was, wondered if she had searched for him. He wished he'd been able to leave her some kind of message. What must she think of him? What was she doing now? He missed the way she had treated him like a whole man, not like some handicapped fool who needed to be coddled like a child.

The continued absence of Dogma also bothered him more with each passing day. Until this forced separation, she had been with Jordan nearly every moment of every day for uncounted years. Lorelei had assured him that the great beast was being well-looked after and seemed happy in the barn with the cult's other animals, but he fretted over her absence more each day.

One sunny morning while sitting by the waterfall, Lorelei was called away. One of the young acolytes had injured herself badly and apparently Lorelei was the only temple member with medical training.

Lorelei told Jordan he had to return with her, but he

asked her to leave him by the waterfall to enjoy one of the last warmish fall days, promising that he wouldn't wander off and he would sit there until she returned. Soon the snows would confine him indoors and he wanted to be out as much as possible, he pleaded.

How ironic, Jordan mused after Lorelei left him. Before he met Sydney he felt frightened of the outdoor world. Now he couldn't get enough of it.

Did Sydney know that he loved her and wanted to marry her? Had he told her how much she meant to him? Or had he played the fool and kept his feelings to himself? He couldn't remember. A heavy weight filled his chest and pressed on his lungs, making it hard to draw a breath.

"Jordan? Are you okay?"

Jordan had forgotten all about Lorelei. He forced a smile and told her he'd be fine sitting alone. After a few moment's hesitation Lorelei agreed and ran off to care for the injured girl, leaving Jordan to wallow in the unexpected luxury of time alone outdoors.

He leaned back against the boulder he had come to think of as "his spot" and gazed at the faint auras of the trees and plants that grew around the pool at the base of the waterfall. The sound of water tumbling over rocks and into the pool gradually quieted his thoughts and filled him with a sense of peace.

He smelled the faint sweetness of early decay. A sure sign of fall, Lorelei had recently informed him, and he lifted his face to the sun. He might not be able to see sunlight but he could feel its warmth on his cheeks.

"You there, who are you?" A man's voice sounded gruff and gravelly–not unfriendly, but not welcoming either.

Jerked out of his drowsy state, Jordan opened his eyes and saw an aura standing on the opposite bank of the stream. Another man! He jumped to his feet and shouted "Hello!"

"Quiet you fool, you want the women to hear you? Follow the path above the waterfall and you'll find a bridge. I'll meet you at the top."

"I cannot," replied Jordan. It wasn't only that he had to stay where he was and wait for Lorelei's return; the risk of slipping and falling into the rushing stream and being swept away was too great a danger.

The aura wheeled and disappeared into the trees. A great depression swept over Jordan and he sat back down. He drew his knees up, wrapped his arms around them, and rested his forehead on them. The first man he had met since leaving Graceville was gone. He didn't even have the chance to ask him about the temple and Mallory Dunne, and where the hell were they anyway?

"Who are you?" The voice came from his left. Jordan's head snapped up and he saw the aura standing nearby. He scrambled to his feet again.

"I'm Jordan James. I'm sorry, I'm staying at the Temple of Gaia and I'm blind and I couldn't try to find the bridge or I would've come to you." His words tumbled over one another, trying to explain to this man before he left him alone again.

Jordan felt the man relax, felt a hand touch him briefly on the shoulder. The hand followed his arm down, grasped Jordan's hand and shook it. It was a large hand, rough and strong. Jordan felt healed scars on the thumb pad. He held onto the hand longer than was polite, then reluctantly let it drop. He had the insane urge to pick it up again and curled his hands into fists to stop himself. The man would think him a fool.

"Sorry, son. There's no need to apologize. My name is

Michael Keene but most folks call me Big Mike. Where are you from and how did you end up at the temple?"

"I'm from Iowa, here by way of Nebraska. A group of Mallory Dunne's acolytes found me camping and brought me here. Wherever here is."

"You were traveling alone? In the mountains? That's downright foolish of you, a blind man alone in the wilderness. Don't you know there are dangerous creatures out here? Not to mention the acolytes. You'd be safer in a town with other people."

Jordan hesitated. Big Mike might be trustworthy, but then again, he might not. He couldn't take the risk of telling him about Sydney. What if Mike passed the information on to Mallory?

"I have a large guide dog. Unfortunately the acolytes took her from me. You're the first man I've met since I arrived. Where are all the other men? Do they have their own separate compound?"

Big Mike gave a choked laugh. "Yeah, they have their own compound all right, an underground compound."

Jordan frowned. "I don't understand. Do they live in some sort of survival shelter?" He had heard about the bomb and doomsday shelters that people had once constructed in their backyards when fears of atomic war had run high. The government had even constructed large underground complexes to house the most valued politicians and necessary staff.

Perhaps some wealthy citizen had built himself a shelter here in the mountains.

Big Mike snorted. "Around here, unless you're a female, your life isn't worth spit. The males are either sent to the mines or a lucky few get to saw down trees and cut and haul firewood."

"Are you a woodcutter then?"

"Yeah, I'm a woodcutter. I'm one of the lucky ones, big and strong and they had just lost a cutter to a widow maker when they picked me up."

Jordan was trying to stay focused on getting useful information but he had to ask. "What's a widow maker?"

"Sometimes trees don't fell properly and they get hung up. Or a big blow will knock over a weak or old tree and leave it leaning until either its own weight or something else makes it fall. This one came down on top of a guy and crushed him. His bad luck, my good fortune. I was headed for the mines and got a reprieve."

Big Mike's voice grew thoughtful. "I wonder what the High Bitch wants with you. It's not like her to keep extra mouths around unless they serve a purpose. And since you're blind I doubt that she'll use you for breeding stock. She likes her male babies big to work the mine and her females perfect. She's a bit like a Nazi, trying to create her own superior race."

Jordan shrugged. He didn't understand what Big Mike was talking about. "Maybe she's just giving me a place to stay until spring and then she'll send me on my way."

This time Big Mike barked out a real laugh and slapped Jordan lightly on the shoulder. "Yeah, good one, but no. Queen Mallory does not like men. If she's feeding and housing you she has something in mind for you. I can promise you that. Especially as she's letting you stay in the retreat with all her precious lambs. She can't send you into the mines or out to cut wood, you'd be of no use blind. Besides, she only keeps three woodcutters on at a time and we're still healthy enough to work."

Jordan had so many questions he didn't know what to ask first. "What kind of mines? Is that where all the men are?"

Understanding began to dawn in Jordan's brain. He didn't like what it implied. "Is that what you meant by an underground compound? The men are all living in old mines?"

Big Mike grunted what Jordan took as an affirmative. The man made more noises in his conversation than Jordan had ever heard anyone use. Not even the crown prince of Gravakia, who snorted, chortled, and wheezed his way through any conversation could compare.

"Are they digging for something in the mines or are they being held prisoner there?" he asked.

"Both. The Bitch sends the men into the mines to dig for gold. There are three abandoned mines in the area and she has crews working all three. Her great-great grandfather laid claim to them in the mid eighteen hundreds. He took the easy gold and closed the mines down. Mallory came here right after the world went to hell and reopened them."

"You're pulling my leg. Are they actually finding gold in the abandoned mines? And why do the men stay? Sounds hokey to me."

Big Mike's voice grew rough and angry. "It's not a joking matter, son. And it isn't just grown men, she exploits male children as well. Mallory takes the boys from their mothers as soon as they turn five and sends them to work alongside the men. Anyone who goes into the mine only comes out on a stretcher, dead. And yeah, they're finding enough gold to make her think the wasted lives are worth it."

If Big Mike was telling Jordan the truth then Mallory Dunne was a dangerous, and possibly deranged, woman. "I don't understand. Why does Mallory want gold? You can't eat it. There's no place left to spend it. It doesn't make sense."

Big Mike clapped a hand on Jordan's shoulder and squeezed gently. "Think about it. Gold has always been coveted and hoarded. It's a sign of wealth, power, and prestige. Ancient civilizations worshipped it: the Egyptians, the Aztecs–remember King Midas? History is rife with tales of gold. Rapunzel spun straw into gold, alchemists spent their lives and fortunes looking for the magic formula to turn ordinary metals into gold. Wars are fought over gold. The search for gold drove the westward expansion of the United States."

Jordan frowned. "So you're telling me that you believe Mallory wants power and is willing to sacrifice men and children to get it. If that's true then why does she want me?"

"*That's* what I'm trying to get you to understand. Besides woodcutting and working the mines there's only one reason Mallory brings a man into the temple. But you're blind so she wouldn't use you. Damn. Here comes Lorelei."

Big Mike pulled his hand from Jordan's shoulder. "Sorry, I have to go before she spots me or I'll find myself digging in a mine. Watch yourself, Jordan. Mallory Dunne is not to be trusted, no matter how lovely she is. She's all honey-sweet beauty on the outside and conniving Ice-Queen on the inside. She wants you for something, mark my words."

Panic made Jordan's pulse beat faster. Not only was Big Mike the first male he had encountered since arriving at the temple, he was also an important source of information, something that Jordan desperately yearned for. Being blind meant he couldn't judge the people and happenings around him because they never spoke in his presence. He couldn't observe them, couldn't listen to the nuances of their words. Mallory Dunne had placed him in a carefully controlled vacuum within the temple.

"Wait! Please don't leave yet, he begged. "Take me with you. I don't belong here and I have more questions. I need to know more about this place."

Big Mike was already climbing the trail beside the waterfall. "Sorry bucko, no can do. It's not worth my hide if I get caught. I'll try to catch you alone again." The next moment his aura disappeared upstream.

Jordan stood staring after him, dazed by what he had learned. He was still standing when Lorelei returned.

"Did I see you with someone?" She asked when she reached Jordan's side, her voice sharp with suspicion.

Jordan turned around and gave her what he hoped was an innocent smile. "Nope, you must have imagined it. I thought I heard a deer. Maybe that's what you saw. I'm ready to go back to my room now. Is the injured girl going to be okay?"

Lorelei didn't speak for a long moment. Jordan felt her scrutinizing him, trying to tell if he was lying. Finally she gave him a short answer and herded him back to the retreat.

Jordan felt relieved when he was locked alone in his room later that day. He needed to think about what he had learned. He had known that the Temple of Gaia only housed females, but he had assumed that they simply turned men away. Thanks to Big Mike, he now knew that they trapped the men and forced them to work in one of Mallory's mines.

For the first time he understood that he was in danger. Big Mike was right, if Mallory was housing and feeding him she had an ulterior motive. He would be worthless as a miner or woodcutter so she must be saving him for some other purpose. But for what? Why did the High Priestess need a blind piano man?

Jordan thought back over the conversation with Big Mike. He had said something about breeding. What was it? That Jordan didn't have to worry because of his blindness. Why would—oh no.

He jumped to his feet and began pacing the room. He shook his head. *No.* The whole idea was too preposterous to even contemplate.

Then again, here he was, living in a temple surrounded by fifty or more young women while the men and children mined gold for a woman who had anointed herself High Priestess.

Jordan stopped in the center of the room and fisted his hands at his sides. Was it possible? Had he been brought here to provide stud services to the temple acolytes, like a prize bull or stallion?

And afterwards? If he agreed–and he wouldn't–what then? Would they kill him outright? Sacrifice him on an alter? Or would they leave him alone in the forest to slowly starve to death? Or worse, get eaten by some wild animal?

The thought of having sex with women he didn't know made him feel slightly nauseated. He knew there were men who would leap at the opportunity but he was not one of them. When he was on the concert circuit there had been girls who offered themselves to him but he had always turned them down. He didn't want to hurt anyone's feelings so he was polite about it, but he never felt tempted.

Maybe his reluctance to become involved with a woman had been tied to his blindness. And maybe his sister Torrie was partly responsible. She had taught him about women's feelings and their need to feel appreciated and cared for, stressing that their need for a relationship went beyond the physical.

Even without his sister's lectures Jordan had learned that he needed to feel emotionally connected to feel desire. And his emotional connection was with Sydney. He'd rather face the forest alone than betray his love for her. The High Bitch would have to look elsewhere for her stud.

Then he remembered that Big Mike had brushed him aside as a candidate because of his blindness. Relief washed through Jordan. He was safe. Mallory wouldn't risk breeding blind children that would be of no use to her.

His relief was short-lived when he remembered that Mallory had asked Jordan if he had been born blind and he had told her no.

6

SYDNEY STEADILY MADE her way north. Her hair had grown out enough to become a nuisance and she began to wear it in a short braid. She had hacked off her braid six months earlier after a man, one of the Desperate Ones, had captured her by her braid and held her prisoner.

Before she cut her hair, her thick, black braid had reached below her hips. Today the simple act of braiding her much shorter hair made her feel as if she had recovered a small piece of the self-confidence that had been stolen from her.

The nights were growing noticeably colder. The last two mornings she had awakened to a crunchy white frost edging the leaves and grass. She dug out one of her wool sweaters and began to sleep in her long underwear. The hens fluffed their feathers to keep warm and she took to covering their cages with pine boughs at night to help them conserve heat.

The leaves had fully turned and the mountainsides went from a multitude of shades of green to a colorful collage of reds, browns, and yellows interspersed with the deep green of spruce and pine. It was breathtakingly beautiful and she wished she had someone to share it with.

She welcomed the icy bite of the frosty air as she sucked it deep into her lungs. It made her feel clean and wholesome and helped wash away some of the self-loathing she still carried inside.

The nightmare of her twin's murder faded into the background. It wasn't gone by any means–she would never forget that awful day and her role in it–but the beauty that surrounded Sydney reminded her that life went on.

Every step she took carried her closer to Smokey.

Closer to Smokey. The phrase became her mantra. She became the little engine that could, chugging up and down the slopes, only stopping when she ran out of daylight.

She hugged the lower slopes of the mountains as much as possible, only climbing high to circle around civilization. Like the big cities in the east, Colorado's cities appeared to be mostly deserted. With the lifelines of the trucking industry broken it was impossible for city-dwellers to find food on the grocery shelves. Only the smaller farming towns and the single households that knew enough to plant vegetable gardens and hunt game had survived.

Sydney often spotted people near the smaller towns but managed to avoid being seen. Now that she no longer had Jordan and Dogma with her she felt vulnerable once again. Too many people had lost the thin veneer of civilization. Their lives hanging by a slender thread, the search for food became all that mattered. People could no longer be trusted to behave in a proper manner, to respect a young woman's rights. She felt safest not letting anyone get too close.

Occasionally she climbed above the tree line and used her binoculars to search the land below. She didn't like to do it too often as it ate up a full day and took a great deal of effort, but it helped her track her northward progress.

She felt a sense of delight and accomplishment the afternoon she spotted Fort Collins, the last city between Denver and Cheyenne, Wyoming. She was closing in on the Wyoming border. The knot she carried in her chest since Jordan's departure eased a little. In another two days she should be in the land of Smokey's people.

Sydney put away her binoculars and hiked down into the trees. She stopped to let Ginny and Henrietta have some free time scrounging for late season insects. Any day now the snows would come and they'd have nothing to eat. The hens would slowly starve to death and there was nothing she could do about it.

Jordan's sister Torrie had grown corn for her chickens, dried and cracked it and fed it to them through the Iowa winter. Unless Sydney found a supply of some type of grain she would be forced to butcher the two hens who had become her only friends and companions. The thought thoroughly depressed her. She was going to end up betraying the hen's trust and she couldn't see any way to prevent it.

Two days later she awoke to a solid mass of low leaden clouds that stretched from horizon to horizon and obscured the mountaintops. Around mid-morning it began to snow; large, fat flakes that fell softly and immediately clumped together. The flakes began to accumulate and swirl around her feet.

She stopped to cover the shivering, unhappy hens with her rain cloth, placing both hens next to one another in one cage. She tied the cage off the back of her pack instead of one to each side. The hens were crowded but they would be warmer huddled together.

She left the second cage behind. It was unlikely she would ever need it again.

Later that day Sydney dug out a red and white knit wool hat that her mother had made for her years earlier and matching mittens, then snapped her down vest over her wool sweater. She resisted the urge to pile on more clothes. It was important not to overdress and grow sweaty. The sweat would chill her and possibly bring on hypothermia and she no longer possessed the body fat to recover from hypothermia.

Sydney dropped lower and lower in elevation until she hiked along a river that meandered between the peaks of the Medicine Bow Range and the high desert to the east. The snowfall was lighter here, the flakes smaller and icier, the north wind fierce with nothing to block it. The snowflakes hurt when they hit her face but at least they didn't pile up into impassable drifts.

She put one foot in front of the other, kept her head down, and plodded northward. She refused to dwell on her predicament, on what would happen if the snow continued to pile up before she reached her friend's home. There was only each step: left foot, right foot, left foot, right foot. Each step took her two feet closer to her destination.

With her head down, her brain focused only on each footfall and the river to her right, she almost walked into the town of Woods Landing. When the town's road sign nearly grazed her temple she snapped out of her stupor. She jerked to a halt and stared stupidly at the sign, trying to make sense of the words. Woods Landing Resort to the west, Woods Landing to the north.

A town. She mustn't walk into a town. Towns were full of danger.

She looked around her and realized that the river ran alongside a snow-covered highway, a highway she had been following for a while without even realizing.

"Have to be a little more alert, Sydney girl. Walking with your eyes on your feet is stupid. Anyone could've come along this road and attacked you." Her voice sounded strange to her ears, hoarse and husky, as if her voice box had rusted. She wondered if a person's voice disappeared from lack of use the way muscles atrophied with lack of exercise.

It was time for a break. She veered away from the river into a thick stand of spruce trees. She covered her face with her hands and pushed her way through the stiff branches until she stood in the center of the trees. Thick with needles, the branches blocked the wind and created a welcome oasis from the storm.

Sydney removed her pack, checked on the hens, and pulled her maps out of the back pocket. It was a good thing the sign had pulled her out of her trance, she realized as she studied the Wyoming map. The Laramie River changed direction just north of Woods Landing and headed east toward its namesake. She would have been taken miles out of her way if she had continued to mindlessly follow it.

She stepped outside of the trees and studied the sky. The low gray clouds still stretched in a solid mass as far as she could see to the north. The peaks on either side of the river were obscured. She could see no indication that the storm would let up soon. How long had she been walking into the biting wind? It felt like days but it had only started snowing that morning.

She pulled off a mitten and pressed her fingers to her cheeks and nose but couldn't feel her touch. Hoping she wasn't too late to avert frostbite, she reentered the spruce trees and dug into her pack and pulled out a long woolen scarf. She buried her nose in the scarf for a brief moment. It still carried the scent of the cedar trunk where she had once kept it stored during the summer months.

Her twin sister Shannon had sheared, cleaned, and spun the wool from their grandfather's sheep, dyed it a glorious sea green to match Sydney's eyes, and woven the scarf on her small homemade loom.

A gift of love. Sydney dashed the tears from her face before they could freeze and wrapped the scarf around her neck and over her face and nose, leaving only her eyes exposed.

She stepped out of the trees and again searched the landscape before her. Everything she could see was either gray or blanketed in white. The stiff wind drove the snow sideways and pushed sparse tufts of grass to the ground.

She needed to head west, but without the river to guide her she could easily get lost if she tried to push on. Waiting out the storm was the only sensible thing to do. She turned and plunged back into the trees, suddenly anxious to escape the wind and the gray.

Sydney pulled her knife and hacked some spruce branches from low on two of the south side trees, then lay them on the bare ground underneath. The thick needles kept the snow from reaching the ground and would provide good cover from the storm. She set her pack on the boughs, apologized to the chickens for not letting them out, and cut more branches and piled them next to her pack.

She pulled out her sleeping bag and crawled into it, pulled the extra branches over her body, the hens, and her pack, and fell immediately to sleep.

When she awoke and pushed the spruce boughs aside she sensed the storm had wore itself out. The wind no longer howled through the trees. Sydney lay in her bag, cozy and warm and rested. And very, very hungry. Her stomach growled in protest at being neglected.

Unable to ignore the gnawing ache in her belly any longer, she crawled out of her bag, grabbed a hen under each arm and took them down to the stream for a drink. The sun shone in a deep blue sky. Puffy white clouds sailed overhead. Snow sparkled on every surface and fractured into colorful prisms. Her breath condensed into a vapor cloud in the crisp, cold air. Winter had arrived.

The water was so cold it hurt her teeth but she drank all she could hold. She had nothing else to offer her empty stomach.

When she stood, black shadows passed over her eyes and she swayed. She tried to remember when she had last eaten. Must be days ago. Maybe three? Two eggs, the last two the hens had laid for her. They were hungry too, she knew. If they didn't find Smokey soon they would all die.

She made her way slowly back to the stand of spruce, willing the dizziness to go away. The most difficult part of her journey lay ahead of her. She thought that Smokey's family lived on the western slopes of the Medicine Bow Mountains, and she was on the eastern side of the range. She had to find a way over the mountains.

The thing that worried her the most however, was that she didn't know exactly where Smokey lived. When she had asked him, a lifetime ago now, he had only given her the general location. She could be nearing her destination, or have another week's travel. She hoped it wasn't the latter because she would never make it.

Sydney pushed the thought from her mind and checked her map again. She decided to do something she had avoided since leaving her grandfather's farm. She would follow a road over the mountains: Highway Forty-seven. Following a road would eat up less of her remaining energy. Plus it had the added bonus of following Fox Creek so she'd have ready water available.

There were dangers involved with walking a road, mainly an increased chance of running into people, but given her weakened state it was a risk she had to take. Mind made up, she filled her water bottles and set off.

The land rose steeply on both sides of the highway. Sydney imagined herself walking the bottom of the letter u, crisscrossing from one side to the other. The north wind hadn't penetrated most of the narrow valley and she soon found herself wading through shin-deep snow. She stopped to dig out her rain pants and pulled them over her jeans. It was important to stay dry.

She had to sit down to pull on the waterproof pants and nearly didn't get up again. She felt so weak and tired. Her stomach ached and gnawed at her until she felt as if she had turned into nothing more than a big, empty shell.

What she wouldn't give for a plate of her mother's homemade pasta with meatballs and red sauce. Or breakfast! She loved breakfast. Waffles with maple syrup and bacon or ham steak with cheesy scrambled eggs. Her mother's homemade Anadama bread slathered with butter and homemade strawberry jam. Shoot, right now she'd settle for the awful noodlekugel her sister had made once.

Left foot, right foot. Before long she found herself staggering. By late afternoon Sydney knew she wasn't going to make it but she refused to stop. She no longer took steps, it was more of a stumbling forward.

Twice she fell to her knees and had to argue herself to her feet. She swayed, got turned around, walked fifty yards back the way she had come, realized she was going the wrong way, cried over the backward progress and turned again.

Eventually she simply stood in the center of the highway, unable to take another step. How long could she remain on her feet? What would happen to the hens? They were trapped in their cage. She should at least set them free and give them a fighting chance at survival.

Sydney dropped to her knees and slipped out of her pack. Large black spots swam in front of her eyes, making it hard to find the knots that held the cover on the hen's cage.

She swore in frustration with her clumsy fingers and shook her head, trying to clear the spots away but they multiplied. It was like when she looked at the sun and then away and saw a black spot, as if her retina had been burned out by the sun's glory.

The sun's glory. At least she would die out here under the sky and sun and not underground, not in a dark cave. She gave up on the knots, fell forward on top of her pack and closed her eyes. It was a pretty valley, a good place to die.

Meet your death with a song in your heart. She had read that once somewhere. Or was it one of Smokey's wisdoms? What was her song? A terrible sadness came over her. She had no song of her own. She hadn't lived long enough to find her song. How could she die without a song?

It was her last thought before she slipped into the dark void.

7

Jordan couldn't get Big Mike out of his mind. He replayed their conversation over and over, trying without success to glean more information from it. He wanted to demand the truth from Lorelei, but he suspected she would give him nothing and he would only endanger Big Mike's freedom.

Another week passed, and while he waited for Big Mike to show up at the falls, he was never left alone except when he was locked in his room. He realized that the opportunity for another meet with the woodcutter was unlikely and if he wanted to learn more about what Mallory had in store for him he was going to have to do it himself.

He started his campaign the following morning while walking to the falls with the guide he now knew was a guard.

"I'm impressed with how well the temple is managed, Lorelei," he began, "Although I can't see, it smells clean and we certainly eat well. Do you feed me special meals, or do all the women eat what I eat?" He had chosen the exact right note to hit. Lorelei's heartfelt enthusiasm for her leader was clear.

"Mallory does a wonderful job, doesn't she? We all eat the

same meals. We raise meat and vegetables and corn and beans for drying. Also wheat for baking. We have members who preserve fresh produce for the winter months and several who can slaughter and process the meat. We eat more stews and soups during the winter of course, but there's plenty and it's tasty. No one starves in the Temple of Gaia."

"I'll agree with that," said Jordan. He wondered how well the miners were fed. He suspected they were given just enough to keep them alive. "Obviously I can't see the temple, but I sense that it is quite large. How do you heat it during the colder months?" If he could get her talking about firewood he might also hear about the woodcutters.

"We have two wood furnaces in the lowest level that heat the temple. In the summer we spread out and use all the rooms, but during the coldest months we all move down to the first level and share rooms, usually two to a room. We shut off the upper two levels to conserve heat. The High Priestess needs her privacy to meditate and make plans for the rest of us so she has a suite of rooms. And you won't have to share with anyone obviously."

Ahh, so Mallory must be planning to keep him around for at least part of the winter, thought Jordan, relieved. Good to know.

"Wow!" he said aloud. "You cut wood on top of everything else! You must have some very strong and fit women in the temple."

Tell me about the woodcutters, Lorelei, he silently begged. Tell me about Big Mike. Where do they live? How many men are there?

"Oh, no. Cutting down trees is dangerous work and more than we choose to handle," Lorelei answered. "We barter with some local men for wood. They keep us supplied in exchange for a share of our food."

This was the opening Jordan had been waiting for. "Speaking of men, I haven't heard any male voices in the temple. Am I the only one in residence at the moment? Do the men have their own temple nearby?"

"There are no other men." Lorelei's tone was curt.

Uh-oh. Hit a nerve there. Time to change the subject. "How much land does the temple own? It must be a large acreage to support all the members. I wish I could see it, the falls sound lovely."

"It is lovely. Most of it anyway. There're some old mines with piles of slag that are ugly but they're on the other side of the ridge so we can't see them from here. As for how much land the temple owns I can't answer that. Most of the land has been in Mallory's family for several generations."

"Really? How nice for her. Someone in her family must have built the hotel that she calls the Temple of Gaia now."

"Nooo, I don't think so." Lorelei's tone sounded somewhat guilty.

"Don't think so what?" asked Jordan.

"I'm pretty sure Mallory found the hotel abandoned after the upheaval and she just sort of moved in." Lorelei sounded defensive. "The place was empty. Mallory did nothing wrong."

"Ahhh, I see." Jordan needed to calm Lorelei's defensiveness or she'd stop talking. "I agree, Mallory did nothing wrong. I'm pretty sure that's called claiming squatter's rights. I'm sure no one cares, especially if it was abandoned when she found it."

Despite his effort, Lorelei decided she'd been talking too much. "Enough questions. It's time to return to your room." She took Jordan's arm, turned him away from the falls, and took him back to his room without speaking another word.

Two weeks later an acolyte named Ruby came to Jordan's room to escort him on his morning walk. When Jordan asked after Lorelei he learned the young woman who had been injured several weeks earlier had taken a turn for the worse. Lorelei was staying by her side to keep an eye on her.

Ruby's voice sounded younger than Lorelei. After Lorelei's habitual reticence, Ruby's constant chatter wore on Jordan, but he recognized an opportunity to learn more about the workings of the temple when one came along.

"Ruby. What a pretty name. Do the acolytes choose their own names when they join the temple?"

Ruby giggled. "Thank you. Miss Mallory lets us choose if we want. Some of the girls keep their names but I was happy to get a new name. I hated the name my parents chose. Harriet. Ugh. Who names their daughter Harriet? Just because it was my grandmother's name, and her mother before her. Some traditions are meant to be broken. I chose Ruby because it's my favorite color and it's also a jewel."

"Good choice. I know what you mean about family names. I'm named for my maternal grandfather, but fortunately I don't mind the name Jordan. How long have you lived in the temple?"

"Oh, I've been here almost four years. The older acolytes make a sweep of the towns and cities once a year and pick up any suitable orphans they find. I came from Fort Collins way. My momma and daddy died early on. I was living on the streets and waiting to join them when the temple found me, so I'm real thankful Miss Mallory took me in. I have a good life here."

Jordan wondered how far Fort Collins was from the temple. How far did the acolytes roam looking for new recruits? He doubted Ruby could answer that. She seemed pleasant enough, but not terribly intelligent. She was indeed fortunate the temple had taken her in. He wondered if he could learn anything useful from her.

"What happens to the orphan boys that they find?" he asked. Jordan desperately wanted to know about the men. How many were there? "I haven't heard any male voices since I've been here." *Other than Big Mike.* But he knew better than to mention the woodcutter.

"Oh, we have young boys in the nursery. But Miss Mallory takes them to the men's temple when they turn five years old. It's hard on some of the mothers, but mostly we know it's going to happen and Miss Mallory says it prevents any problems down the road."

Jordan looked at her in surprise. Ruby had a petite aura, clear and bright. Honest. She believed she was telling him the truth. Apparently Mallory didn't mind lying to her acolytes. Were the mines a secret? "There's a nursery?" he asked aloud. "Where do the babies come from?"

Ruby giggled again. "Didn't anyone ever tell you about the birds and bees, Master Jordan?"

Jordan flushed. "Yes, Ruby, I know about the birds and the bees. What I'm asking is, if there are only women in the temple, how does anyone get pregnant? Or are the women pregnant when they're brought here? Or do the woman visit with the men's temple?"

Ruby's giggle sounded a little breathless this time. "Sometimes the acolytes bring a pregnant women here, but mostly the women of breeding age get to participate in the Solstice Ceremony. I turned sixteen a couple months ago so this will be my first time."

Jordan furrowed his brow. "I've heard of the solstice, but never the Solstice Ceremony," he said slowly. "Are we talking about the winter solstice, the shortest day of the year?"

"Uh-huh. Miss Mallory says it's the shortest day but I never measured it myself. I trust her to know. She's very smart, being the High Priestess and all."

"Sooooo, the temple holds a Solstice Ceremony...," prompted Jordan.

Ruby's aura bounced. "I can't wait. Miss Mallory schedules the breeding so the babies are born in September after the hard work of summer is finished. That way the work gets done and the mamas can concentrate on their babies over the winter."

A small knot was beginning to form in Jordan's stomach. "Sounds...interesting. " It sounds insane, he wanted to shout at Ruby. But Ruby wasn't the one who was insane and it wouldn't be right to shout at her. She was only an ignorant girl being duped by the High Bitch.

"How many babies were born this year?" he asked instead.

"Oh, we had a good year. We had thirty new babies. Everyone of breeding age who didn't breed the year before participates, but not everyone gets pregnant. We should have had thirty-one but one girl died this year while trying to deliver her baby. Lorelei says that's a rare occurrence. The girl was a skinny little thing. She looked like a little girl and Lorelei says the baby was just too big for her. I won't have that problem on account of I have nice wide hips. Miss Mallory says I'm built for breeding." The note of pride in Ruby's voice was unmistakable.

Jordan was having trouble finding his tongue. Thirty babies? And more than that tried to get pregnant? Good lord. He wondered how last year's chosen one had felt after all that...work.

The thought boggled his mind and made him feel a little nauseated. He tuned back into Ruby's chatter.

"...plus you're not built as big as Mike Keene. Mr. Keene is *really* tall and he's big all over. And I mean all over." She giggled again. "I heard some of the girls talk about his, uh... well," she paused. "You should see his hands, they make a big pumpkin look small," she finished lamely.

"Wait, did you say Mike Keene?"

Big Mike was last year's sperm donor? No wonder he knew so much about it. Why hadn't he told Jordan? Then again, was that something a man would confess to a stranger? Or anyone else for that matter? Yes, a lot of men liked to brag about their sexual conquests, but any decent man would feel violated at being treated like a prize bull. He didn't blame Mike Keene one bit for not telling him.

"His name's Mike Keene but most of the girls call him Big Mike. Do you know him?"

"No. I thought the name sounded familiar, but that's because I knew someone named Mike Kern from back in Iowa." *Careful Jordan. Don't give Mike away.*

He needn't have worried. Ruby was barely listening to him.

"Some of the girls were afraid of him cause he's so big and it was their first time and all, but I won't be afraid. Besides, I don't think you'd ever hurt anyone. You're nice. And built good. You're very manly with a nice chest and strong legs and you have good muscles. That's important you know. Strong men have the best chance of surviving and providing for others so women naturally want to mate with them. Miss Mallory explained all about evolution and survival of the fittest to us. Plus you're handsome too. You'll make pretty babies." She giggled again.

"What? Me? You must be mistaken. Mallory hasn't said anything to me about making babies."

Big Mike had brushed aside the possibility of Jordan being this year's stud because he was blind. Mike had implied that Mallory wouldn't knowingly breed handicapped children.

Only Big Mike didn't know that Jordan hadn't been born blind. Jordan again remembered his first conversation with Mallory, when she asked about his blindness. He had told her it was the result of a car accident and she had sounded relieved. Pleased even.

His breath stuttered in his chest.

According to Ruby, Mallory had chosen him to be this year's sperm donor. His stomach roiled and he fisted a hand against his belly.

Would Big Mike have told Jordan more about the Solstice Ceremony if he had known that Jordan was this season's Chosen One? Frustration washed over him.

He desperately wanted to talk with Big Mike again, but whenever he left his room he was kept under close watch. Mallory had made him her prisoner, soon to be a pawn in her scheme to produce more workers for her mine.

Jordan balled his hands into fists. Somehow he had to find a way to sneak off and find Big Mike.

A warm hand patted his arm and pulled him out of his reverie.

"Are you okay, Master Jordan?" Ruby giggled her little girl laugh. "Don't worry, we won't jump you all at once. It's done in a very orderly manner over almost a week's time. Some of the girls told me all about it. You'll do fine, I'm sure of it."

Jordan forced his fists to relax and patted the hand on his arm before removing it. "Thank you, Ruby, that's very, ah… reassuring. I think I'd like to go back to my room now."

He didn't tell his escort that he felt faint at the thought of the Solstice Ceremony and his part in it. Didn't tell her that he was in fact a virgin himself and the thought of servicing—he couldn't think of any other word for it—servicing dozens of women made him want to run away screaming and take his chances in the forest.

8

Low voices pulled Sydney from her dream. She fought consciousness, preferring to remain with her mother and sister in the sunny vegetable garden. They were planting marigolds in amongst the vegetables to deter hungry insects. Sydney loved to work in the garden with her mother. The sun-warmed dirt smelled so good. Planting time was a time of hope.

Then Shannon hugged her and whispered in Sydney's ear that it was time for her to go. Her mother waved and smiled and blew a kiss. Sydney reached out her arms to grasp them both but they faded from her mind.

"I don't think she's going to make it."

The voice sounded vaguely familiar but she couldn't place it. Someone from her past maybe. Or someone she'd met since she left Pop's farm. It didn't matter. He was right, she wasn't going to make it. Knowing she didn't have to fight to stay alive freed her. She began to drift again.

"She's young. The young are resilient. She'll make it." The second voice was old and cracked and whispery.

Oh damn. They weren't going to let her go. Sydney struggled to find the strength to beg them to let her die. She wanted to join her family. Wanted to see Shannon and Mama and Daddy and Pops again.

Living was too great a struggle, filled with danger and heartache and tough choices. And loneliness. Her life was filled with pain and loneliness.

Sydney tried to open her eyes but they were too heavy. Tried to move her hand, but despite her best efforts it lay unmoving on top of the rough blanket that covered her.

Blanket? She searched her memory. The last thing she remembered was trying to free Ginny and Henrietta from their cage. She had been in a beautiful steep valley with a creek running through the bottom of it. She had been too weak to untie the knot. Her finger twitched as she remembered tugging at the knots.

Everything had been covered in snow and she had been weak from hunger. She remembered standing in the sunshine, too weak to take another step. Her stomach ached and rumbled. Apparently she was still hungry. If she was hungry then she was still alive. Where was she? Did she walk here in an unconscious state?

"I think she might be coming around."

The whispery rasp sounded close to her right ear. She had heard that voice before, maybe part of a dream that she couldn't quite bring back. Sydney took inventory of her body. Her fingers and toes were throbbing, worse than when they fell asleep and pins and needles woke them up again.

She counted her fingers, moving them slightly one at a time, but got lost at six. She started over and fared no better. It was so hard to focus her attention. She tried and failed to count her toes because she couldn't make them separate enough to count them. It would have to wait until she could sit up and inspect them. She drifted back off, looking for her mother and Shannon.

"Young lady. It's time to wake up."

That voice again, buzzing in her ear, annoying her like the whine of a persistent mosquito. She tried to tell it to go away but her own voice didn't work. She needed to swat it away. Her hand twitched but that's as far as her arm would move.

"Wake up." The voice became insistent.

This time she managed to swallow. "Go 'way." The words were barely more than a breath but apparently her tormenter heard them.

"Get some water."

The voice couldn't be speaking to her. How could she get water? She could barely move her hand. The water was in the river near the trees where she had spent the night and waited out the snowstorm. No, the water ran in the creek at the base of the narrow valley she followed to get to…to get to where? She couldn't think. It took too much energy to think.

She felt a wet rag on her mouth, a few drops squeezed out onto it. She let her mouth fall open and several more drops of water dropped in. She touched her bottom lip with the tip of her tongue, gasped and pulled her tongue back. That couldn't be her lip. It felt rough and scaly and was split by a wide gash.

"Easy. Your lip is split. Open your mouth a little more and I'll let you suck on this wet rag."

Sydney did as requested, weakly sucking the water from

the small bit of cloth. The effort sapped all her energy and she drifted back into her happy dream. Maybe they'd let her die now.

"Young lady, wake up. If you do not eat soon you will die."

I want to die.

Her mother and Shannon faded away. Sydney's consciousness rose up through layers of soft darkness and voids that made her think of the vacuum of space. How could anyone claim that space was a vast emptiness when even a vacuum was something? The question came and went into the void.

"I know you hear me. Come back to the world. You are not finished here yet."

Higher she rose. Sensations began to permeate the stillness of her mind. She was lying on her back. The room was warm. She was in a room! She thought about that for a moment but let it go when she couldn't add to the thought. Her toes and fingers no longer burned but her left pinky finger hurt. So did her feet. Again, she couldn't expand on the impressions so she moved on.

Her stomach hurt. She smelled something cooking; a stew or soup of some kind. It smelled good. She struggled to open her eyes, glimpsed a shadowy figure seated beside her right shoulder and closed them again.

"She's coming around. Maybe this time we can keep her awake long enough to get some broth into her."

Sydney liked the sound of that. Food. But what did the voice mean, "Maybe this time she could stay awake"? Where was she? How did she get here? The last thing she remembered was falling on top of her pack after trying to free the hens from their cage.

The poor hens. Had they made it? Or were they in the soup pot? The idea of eating her friends made her feel ill.

"Wake up, young lady. Open your eyes. You need to eat something." The voice commanded. A voice that was used to being obeyed. "You cannot go back to sleep. You've slept enough. it's time to rejoin the world. There are people who need you."

"Gone. All gone. No one needs me," croaked Sydney. Her voice sounded like a stranger's.

"She speaks! Praise the Great Spirit. Can you open your eyes?"

Sydney opened her eyes but the lids fell closed again. Such effort. Why did she need to open her eyes?

"Try again. You are a strong woman. Be strong."

Why didn't this old woman just go away and leave her alone? But she did as asked, and this time her eyes remained open. Her sight was blurred and she waited for it to clear.

Eventually things began to come into focus, the poles meeting at a peak overhead, the overlapped hides spread over the poles, the thin column of smoke disappearing through an opening near the top.

"Where am I?" It took all her strength to whisper the words.

"You are in my home," answered the old woman.

Sydney turned her head and looked at the woman seated beside her. She looked as old as her voice sounded. Wrinkles deeply creased her round face, reminding Sydney of the dried apple heads she and Shannon had carved one year for an art project. The two long braids that hung over her shoulders were white interspersed with strands of silver gray. It was a face that had seen much. A face that declared hard-won wisdom.

The woman smiled, a gap-toothed smile that pushed up her round cheeks and nearly hid her dark brown eyes. "I am glad you have decided to rejoin the world of the living, young one. Care for some soup?"

Sydney gave a small nod, then hesitated. "Ginny and Henrietta aren't in that pot, are they?" she whispered. "I couldn't eat my friends."

"No, they are not in this pot. I'm sorry, your friends didn't make it. Their metabolism is much faster than ours and the lack of food was more than they could overcome." She hesitated a moment, then shrugged. "I gave them to a family with two small children to feed. Their deaths helped others to survive. It is the way of the world."

She stared at Sydney, waiting. Anger flared in Sydney's breast, then died. Of course it made sense to feed the hens to hungry children. The old woman was right. At least their deaths were put to a good use. She sighed and gave a small nod.

The woman slowly stood. As her eyes took in the woman's moccasins, leggings and buckskin dress, Sydney realized she was lying on the ground. No, not the ground, she amended, she lay on a pile of rushes of some kind covered with furs. Furs. She was in a tepee. Not a modern facsimile made from canvas, but an original covered in hides.

"I am Medicine Woman," said the woman as she sat next to Sydney with a bowl of soup. "Small sips now, your stomach may be hungry but it will rebel."

She supported Sydney's shoulders with one surprisingly strong arm and held the bowl to Sydney's lips. Sydney took a moment to enjoy the enticingly scented steam rising from the bowl, then took a small, cautious sip.

The rich broth coated her tongue and she groaned with pleasure and took another small sip. She almost cried out when Medicine Woman took the bowl away from her lips.

"Slowly. Give your stomach a chance to accustom itself to working again." She sat silently next to Sydney and waited.

Sydney managed several more sips before Medicine Woman took the bowl away. She promised more after Sydney rested and then the woman left the tepee. Sydney closed her eyes and slipped into a deep, healing sleep.

Medicine Woman sat waiting for her when she next awoke. Sydney drank a full bowl of broth this time along with fresh water. By the third time she came awake she felt strong enough to sit up on her own.

Sydney pushed herself up with her hands and placed them in her lap while she waited for the bowl of broth. Her left hand felt strange and she absently rubbed at it, then realized it was bandaged.

"Did I cut myself? I don't remember getting hurt."

"No. You were frostbitten. We had to amputate part of your little finger to prevent the rotting flesh from spreading. You lost both little toes as well."

Horror washed through Sydney. "No! Who gave you permission? You can't just lop off people's body parts!" She pawed at the bandage on her hand.

"I can't believe you caught off my finger. How could you do that? What gave you the right to mess with my body?"

Medicine Woman shrugged, unaffected by Sydney's outburst. "It was the finger or your whole hand, possibly your arm. I made the choice for you as you were incapable of speaking for yourself. You are fortunate the frostbite wasn't worse. You didn't lose your thumb, which allows you to grasp things, and you didn't lose your big toes which help you to balance, nor did you lose an ear or your nose. I'd say the Great Spirit blessed you and you should give thanks. You are alive and relatively unharmed."

Sydney stared at Medicine Woman, unbelieving. Did the

old woman honestly think she should feel grateful? Her perfect whole body, the body she had always taken for granted, was now missing parts. She didn't feel grateful, she felt...deformed.

Sydney finished unwinding the bandage and removed it. A small piece of moss fell out of the bandage. She looked at her hand. The little finger had been amputated at the second joint, leaving a short, red stub. The skin had been pulled over the end and neatly sewn into place. There was no sign of infection.

She replaced the bandage and threw the furs off her body. Both feet were bandaged. She left them alone. She couldn't bear to look at them now that she knew what lay under the bandages.

"You were fortunate," repeated Medicine Woman. "I did the surgery while you were unconscious. The moss prevents infection."

She ladled some soup into a bowl. "Eat this. I have added some meat and corn to the broth. You must start building up your strength." She handed Sydney the bowl and left the tent.

Sydney ate slowly, waiting after every few bites to be sure her stomach was handling the food. She felt off-balance, stunned even, by her missing finger and toes. She thought about the alternative, about freezing to death alone in the narrow valley, or watching her hand and feet turn rotten and foul. By the time she finished the bowl of food she knew that Medicine Woman spoke the truth, she had escaped remarkably unscathed considering how near death she had been.

When the old woman returned she heated water for Sydney to wash and helped her remove her clothes. Sydney struggled to stand, then swayed in place and would have fallen over if Medicine Woman had not grasped her around the waist and placed Sydney's arm over her shoulders.

Medicine Woman was remarkably strong for such a small old woman. Sydney grabbed onto one of the tepee poles for balance while her hostess gently scrubbed the worst of the dirt away with a warm, wet cloth and soap that smelled of sage. It felt good to wash, but she felt embarrassed that someone else had to scrub her like she was a child.

She looked for something to distract her from her humiliation. "Were you always called Medicine Woman? It seems a strange name to give a baby."

"No. My birth name was Singing Sparrow. After my children left and my husband died I came to apprentice with the old medicine woman. When she died I took her place. I belong to the people now. I have no more use for a personal name. I am simply called Medicine Woman."

"I am truly grateful for your help, Medicine Woman. I'm sorry I freaked out earlier. I realize that removing the dead tissue from my body was the right thing to do. Thank you. Please forgive my lack of appreciation earlier."

Medicine Woman's eyes all but disappeared behind her cheek bones as she smiled and giggled. Her giggle sounded like a young woman's. "It was my pleasure."

Sydney returned the smile and felt better than she had in weeks. Medicine Woman helped her into a clean pair of long underwear and led her back to her pallet.

"Sleep now. You will grow stronger each day and then you can tell me your story."

Medicine Woman knew her stuff, observed Sydney two weeks later. Her strength had indeed returned with sleep and regular meals. The bandages were off her hand and feet and the surgical scars were healing. She still grimaced when she looked at them, but they were clean and neat and healthy.

The split on her lip refused to mend, reopening every time she ate or smiled. Fearing infection, Medicine Woman finally decided to stitch it closed, an experience Sydney preferred to forget. Getting sewn up while conscious had been an excruciatingly painful ordeal, one she hoped to never experience again.

Slowly, Sydney and Medicine Woman became accustomed to one another. As Sydney gained her strength back she spent more time sitting with the old woman and talking. She learned that the buffalo numbers were increasing, enough so that the local tribes were able to harvest a few to feed their families through the winter. The buffalo and the deer herds were the people's major source of food.

As she had no man of her own to provide for her, Medicine Woman received meat and hides from the tribe's members in return for providing medical care. She told Sydney that it had taken her several seasons of saving hides before she had collected the number needed to cover a tepee.

Sydney learned that while the men's domain consisted of hunting and providing for their families, the women owned the home. Tepee-making was a chore that traditionally fell to the women. They were also responsible for setting up the tepee, tearing it down, and moving it whenever the food source moved.

Medicine Woman had lived the first half of her life in a tepee, but one covered with canvas, a far inferior covering as it did not insulate against heat and cold. She scowled at the memory when she told Sydney of the old life, then beamed with pride at her hide-covered home.

As Sydney's strength returned she grew restless. One morning Medicine Woman agreed to let her step outside the confines of the tepee.

Sydney couldn't wait to feel the sun on her face again. She rummaged through her pack for heavy socks and outerwear. As this was her first time outdoors since being brought to Medicine Woman she wouldn't be able to spend long outside. Still, she felt excited at the prospect of standing in sunshine and breathing fresh air, and chuckled at how little it took to please her these days.

She pulled on the heavy socks. Her toes no longer filled them out as they once had but she knew she'd been lucky to only lose two. She lightly rubbed the spot where her left little toe once lived. The healing scars were beginning to itch. When she told Medicine Woman about the itches she had smiled and told Sydney it was a sign that all was well with her body.

Sydney was eager to get outside, not only to feel the sun on her face, but also to satisfy her growing curiosity about Medicine Woman's village. Did the villagers all live in tepees like this one? How many were there? Was this a traditional village? Medicine Woman had spoken very little about their surroundings, avoiding Sydney's questions when she asked about the others.

Sydney pulled on her wool sweater, scarf, hat, and mittens, and stepped through the tepee's door flap. She marveled at the heavy, thick buffalo hide that covered the entrance. According to Medicine Woman the buffalo herds were increasing because the ranch cattle that competed with them for food were mostly gone.

It would be at least a century before the land could once again support the great herds that used to roam the plains and western states, if ever, but the buffalo were surviving and reclaiming their rightful place in the eco system.

Sydney stepped clear of the tepee and gasped. She almost turned and staggered back inside to escape the bite of a bitter cold wind and the searing brightness of the sun. She hugged herself against the unexpected cold and blinked until her watery eyes cleared, then took a deep breath and shuffled a step forward, and then another.

It felt good to be walking out of doors again, even if she wasn't eating up the ground in her usual long stride. She was pleased to note that Medicine Woman had been right about losing her little toes. The loss didn't affect her balance at all. She might want to skip sandals next summer though. She laughed aloud at the thought.

The wind snatched her laugh away and the cold made her

split lip burn. She pulled her scarf up over her face before turning to inspect the surrounding landscape.

A snow-covered plain, punctuated by the silvery gray-green of low-growing sage, spread in front of her. Soft purple mountain peaks penned in the plain to the east. The sagebrush and mountains told her that she stood on the edge of a high desert.

She took a deep cleansing breath. The land in front of her possessed a beauty that had been unspoiled by man. With no forest to clearcut for lumber and no water to support a farm or town, the desert plain had been left alone, untouched but for the glaciers that had carved the land during each ice age.

She walked around the tepee and discovered a a small, wooden cabin tucked up against the foot of a mountain. More snowy peaks faded into the haze on either side and beyond.

Smoke curled from the cabin's chimney. The house looked as if it had been hastily constructed with old boards scavenged from elsewhere. Except for the mud that chinked the cracks, it reminded her of the ramshackle shanties of Graceville.

She felt a keen disappointment that Medicine Woman lived in the only tepee and realized how fortunate she was that the old woman shared it with her. It was snug and warm and surprisingly comfortable. Where had the rest of the village gone?

Sydney walked past the cabin, following a path that had been tramped down in the snow. Off to the sides of the trail the unbroken snow stood eight inches deep. She knew it would be deeper on the higher elevations.

She wondered how much snowfall the desert typically received, and if that had changed after the upheaval. Perhaps the desert was receiving more moisture now and changing into a mountain meadow. She wondered if she would be here long enough to learn the answer.

No one came out of the cabin to greet her as she walked by. Other than an occasional creak from the building as the wind buffeted it, she heard only silence. Sydney reached the end of the path and turned to go back to the tepee.

Was the occupant inside staying warm? Were there any children? Was this Medicine Woman's permanent home or was she only here for the winter?

Sydney turned and lifted her face to the sun. It was a winter sun, low in the sky. Although bright it held no warmth, but the sun rays gave her hope for warmer days. She wondered how many days were left until the winter solstice, after which the sun would creep farther north and the days begin to lengthen.

She would have to think about leaving when the snow melted and travel became possible again. But where could she go?

Smokey! Sydney's mouth fell open. She had forgotten all about him. She had left her grandfather's farm to find her friend. The journey had not gone as she had expected. Instead of a straight trek to Smokey's home, or more accurately the general vicinity of Smokey's home as she didn't know *exactly* where he lived, she had made several detours.

She had picked up a blind companion and fallen in love with him. She had helped a town save themselves and made many new friends there. She had fallen into a crazy underground world, helped the King keep his position as ruler of his happy asylum, and made more friends. She knew that she could return to either place and be assured of a welcome.

But before she decided where to go next, she needed to find Smokey. Perhaps Medicine Woman knew of him and where to find him. Smokey would take her into his home, but even more important, he would help Sydney deal with her guilt over the loss of her twin.

Sydney sighed. The guilt she carried because of the way she hid from the danger instead of coming to her sister's aid felt like a giant boulder filling her chest cavity. The weight was hard to breath around and impossible to set aside. Without help it would eventually suffocate her.

She tucked her chin against the wind and slowly headed back toward the tepee. She hated to go inside so soon but her knees were growing wobbly. She had pushed herself far enough today. Tomorrow she would walk again. And every day after that until she felt strong enough to resume her journey.

Relieved to get back to the tepee, she pulled the door flap tight behind her and then stopped short. Medicine Woman had a visitor. Sydney hesitated by the entrance, unsure if she should enter. No one other than Medicine Woman had come into the tepee since Sydney had been there, at least not while she was conscious. While she was unconscious an entire herd of buffalo could have come through and she wouldn't have known it.

Medicine Woman ignored Sydney's presence. Sydney took that to mean she wasn't disturbing anyone. She decided to stay. She quickly removed her outerwear and boots, crossed to her pallet, and sat quietly.

The visitor, a lean-bodied, white-haired man, sat with his back to her. He wore a faded plaid wool shirt and blue jeans. His hair was tied in a short queue. Medicine Woman handed him a bowl of broth, pungent with herbs Sydney didn't recognize. He thanked her softly and slowly drank the contents.

Sydney shifted so her back faced the visitor. If he had come to Medicine Woman for treatment she didn't want to make him uncomfortable. The man said something to Medicine Woman in a smooth, low voice. The voice sounded familiar to Sydney. She thought perhaps he had visited Medicine Woman during the early days of Sydney's recovery, when she had been floating in and out of consciousness.

Satisfied with her theory, Sydney lay down on the pallet with her back to the room and waited patiently for the man to leave. The fire warmed her back and she closed her eyes and dozed. The sound of voices quietly arguing woke her. After a few moments of silence she heard the man get to his feet and thank Medicine Woman. *Good, he's leaving.* She needed to ask the old woman about Smokey.

"Sydney. I want you to meet someone."

Sydney rolled over and faced the pair. The man stood facing away from her.

"This is John. He is the one who found you and brought you to me."

"I'm thankful you found me. I owe you my life, John," said Sydney as she scrambled to her feet to properly shake her savior's hand. The man turned. He towered over her as he dipped his head in shy acknowledgement.

"You owe me nothing. I'm glad I came along when I did. A few more hours and even Medicine Woman, as great as she is, couldn't have brought you back."

Sydney didn't hear his words. A heat wave shot through her and a swarm of hornets buzzed inside her head. Her mouth hung open. A cold shiver racked her body. She took a step toward the man and stopped. *His hair is so white. It can't be.* Then the man raised his head and she looked into a mirror image of her own eyes.

"Oh my god, Dad. I can't believe it's you. Daddy!" And she flung herself into his arms, trying to talk and sob at the same time.

"I can't believe it. You're alive. When you didn't come home we thought you were dead. Shannon and I tried to take care of the farm and Pops but the bad men came and they murdered Shannon and then one killed Pops and I had to leave."

Why wasn't her father hugging her? He stood stiffly, awkwardly patting her back. Wasn't he happy to see her? He must have assumed that she had died in the cataclysms and was now in shock.

She pulled back a little and looked up into her father's eyes, the same slight up tilt, the same soft jade as her own. Her father didn't look happy to see her, or in shock. He looked…confused.

Sydney pulled back a little more and her father's arms dropped to his sides.

"Daddy? What's wrong?"

"John stumbled into one of the nearby camps a few years ago," said Medicine Woman. "Like you, he was not far from dying. I nursed him back to the living but I have been unable to restore his memory. He remembers only waking up in my cabin and nothing before that."

Sydney looked at her father with horror. "You don't remember me?" she whispered. She took a step back and spread her arms. "I'm your daughter, Sydney. I had a twin sister Shannon. Mom was an artist but she died when the tsunamis hit the east coast. You must remember us. You, Mom, Shannon, me, and Pops—Mom's father, we all lived on Pop's sheep farm."

John, *her father!* frowned at her.

Sydney grabbed at his shirt with both hands. "You must remember! We were your family! You took us camping and canoeing. You built radio-controlled airplanes and flew them over the sheep pastures. Pops used to yell at you for that but you'd only laugh and tell him not to worry. You never crashed a plane, you were an awesome flier. You called your fleet of planes Alex Waters Airlines."

Her father continued to look at her, his eyes filled with compassion. Not recognition, compassion. *He felt sorry for her!* Anger and frustration and fear warred in Sydney's chest.

She cast about for something to trigger his memory. Her gaze lit upon her hiking boots. She released her hold on his shirt and ran over to the entrance and picked them up.

She shook the boots in front of his face. "Surely you remember these. You bought these for Mom's birthday because she complained about her old pair. You wrapped them and hid them under your workbench in the basement because you knew Mom would never look there. She always searched for her presents because she couldn't wait until we gave them to her. You teased her about that every birthday and Christmas. It became a game to see if we could hide her presents until it was time for her to open them."

Sydney lowered the boots and fought the tears that threatened to fall. "You never came home and Mom never came home and I found the boots when I was preparing to leave the farm. I thought of them as a special gift from you and Mom together."

She turned away from the stranger who was her father and returned the boots to their spot. "I'm sorry," she said, not looking at him. "I'm being selfish. It must be very difficult to lose your memory."

She forced herself to look at this stranger who was her beloved father. "I'm grateful that you're alive and I'll try to be happy with that." She couldn't say anymore, her throat had closed up.

Her father cleared his throat. "Perhaps we can be friends," he said, his voice gruff with emotion. "I'd like that. I'm sorry I don't remember you; if I had a daughter, I'd want her to be as beautiful and as brave and resourceful as you must be."

Sydney wiped the tears from her face with the back of her hand. She gave her father a watery smile.

"Thank you. So, do they call you John because you're a John Doe? If you're interested, your real name is Alex, Alex Waters. I'm Sydney Waters. Your wife, my mother, was Gabriella. She was very beautiful and a gifted artist. You were madly in love with each other."

John furrowed his brow. "None of that sounds familiar but I'll take your word for it." He gave a decisive nod. "You say my name is Alex. That is the name I will go by. Thank you for giving me an identity. How did I provide for my family?"

Feeling calmer, Sydney stepped closer to the fire, sat, and patted the ground beside her. "You were a field biologist."

Her father joined her and Sydney told him stories of their life together. Medicine Woman sat nearby and listened without speaking. When Sydney's voice began to crack from fatigue her father laid his hand on her shoulder and thanked her, then left.

Sydney remained seated, staring into the small fire that always burned in the tepee. She realized her father must fetch the wood for Medicine Woman's fire and then the thought slipped away. She felt as if she had entered a bizarre new world, a previously unheard of dimension, one in which nothing was as it should be. She recalled a piece she had once read in a science journal written by a group of scientists studying gravity.

The scientists had postulated that the world consisted of layers, like an onion, and that man occupied only one layer. This theory explained why the pull of gravity wasn't as strong as it should be according to the scientist's calculations; the gravity was divided among the layers. Somehow Sydney had slipped off the the layer that contained her world and onto another where there was barely enough gravity to hold her feet to the earth.

She felt eyes upon her and looked up. Medicine Woman's deep brown eyes were filled with concern. "You will become used to it," she said, as if she had heard Sydney's thoughts. "Your father is a good man, that hasn't changed." She spread her hands, as if to warm them over the flames.

"You will build a new relationship with the stranger who is your father. Unless you no longer want him in your life. Your choice. Your future is up to you."

How could she not want him in her life, wondered Sydney?

Before she could voice the question, Medicine Woman rose. "I suggest you rest now. Between your walk and the shock of seeing your father again your body has used a lot of energy. We will talk later."

Sydney nodded. Yes, a nap would help. Her father had survived and somehow they had found each other. She could not let him go now, that much she knew.

10

It was time to stop waiting for something to happen and make something happen himself. Another week had passed since his conversation with Ruby and her startling announcement that he, blind Jordan James, had been chosen to receive the dubious honor of being the temple's next Father of the Year.

He had tried to worm more information from Lorelei, without giving away Ruby's indiscretion. He didn't want to get the young girl in trouble for telling him something he wasn't supposed to know. Despite his broad hints, Lorelei refused to reveal any more of Mallory Dunne's scheme.

He needed his dog back. He not only felt desperate for Dogma's companionship, he would need her if he was to have any chance of escaping the temple. Only Mallory could give permission for him to see Dogma, therefore it was time for him to seek an audience with the temple ruler.

It took him several days to come up with an excuse to see the High Priestess. When he made his request through Lorelei he was forced to wait another two days before Mallory condescended to see him.

High Priestess, my ass. Jordan felt angry at being made to wait. Big Mike had it right–High Bitch was a more accurate title. He forced himself to set his anger aside. When Lorelei showed him to Mallory's chambers his expression showed only concern.

"Yes, Master James. Lorelei tells me you requested an audience in order to share something important?" Mallory's voice was cool but Jordan detected a slight hint of curiosity in her tone. Good.

"Thank you for seeing me, Miss Dunne. First let me tell you how impressed I am with your Temple of Gaia. The place reminds me of the great castles in England. Everything the temple needs is produced right here in the same way the castles produced their own food and cloth. I commend you on your leadership and organizational skills. You should be very proud."

"Oh, you can be sure I am proud of our girls, Master James. Is that all you wished to tell me?" Her voice was impatient and dismissive.

So much for softening her up. Apparently Jordan's opinion mattered not a whit to her. Jordan knew he had to get to the point or lose his opportunity.

"My apologies, Miss Dunne, but I thought your people would have discovered Syd by now." He stood silent and prayed Mallory would take the bait.

"I beg your pardon? Who is Syd? Why should my people discover him?" The sharpness of her tone told Jordan he finally had her full attention.

"Syd was my traveling companion. He was off hunting when your acolytes found me and brought me here." *Forgive me Sydney for making you a man.*

"There was no sign of another man."

"That's because Syd always carried his pack with him. He

didn't trust me. I was his hostage you see. He was taking me to Fort Collins in order to sell me. I was once a well known pianist and singer and Syd figured he could get some gold in exchange for me."

Jordan mentally crossed his fingers. He wished he could see Mallory's expression. He watched her aura carefully for signs of anger or instability.

"That makes no sense. Why would your captor leave you alone in the woods? Why would he give you the opportunity to escape?"

"Not to sound rude, Miss Dunne, but I *am* blind. I cannot make my way through the woods even with my dog. And Syd was afraid of Dogma. He knew he would find me right where he left me when he returned. If you ask the acolytes they'll tell you I was lying on my bed waiting for Syd to return when they found me. If I had been capable of escape I would've been long gone, not hanging around our campsite."

"Why are you telling me this now, Master James?" Mallory sounded curious and suspicious.

"Because I believe Syd is looking for me. I'm worth money to him and he isn't likely to just let me walk away. I think he may have discovered my whereabouts. I had the distinct impression that I was being watched at the falls several days ago. And I felt it two days in a row. I believe it was Syd watching me."

"Really, Master James. Perhaps you are just being paranoid."

Jordan held his breath. He was almost there. She had to believe his plan was all her own idea. *Don't blow it, Jordan.*

He cleared his throat loudly. "Forgive me for disagreeing with you, Miss Dunne, but everyone knows that most blind people develop their other senses. I *know* that someone was watching me and I know it was not an acolyte. The acolytes have a gentleness about them that is unmistakable. *Careful Jordan, don't lay it on too thick.*

"I also know that person meant me harm as I am no longer protected by Dogma. I thought it prudent to warn you. I would feel terrible if one of your girls was hurt if Syd tried to recapture me." *That's enough, Jordan. Let her think it through.*

Mallory thanked Jordan for the warning and dismissed him. Lorelei returned him to his room and told him there would be no trip to the falls later that morning, per Mallory. Jordan sat on his bed and prayed that Mallory was intelligent enough to pick up on his hint that he needed Dogma to protect him, but not concerned enough to send someone looking for sign of Syd.

Several hours later there was a knock and scratching at his door. Jordan stood and braced himself as Dogma leaped onto him and knocked him back several steps. She licked his face furiously and woofed and whined. The room door closed, leaving him alone with Dogma.

He laughed, grabbed her by the ruff, and buried his face in her fur. Her presence gave him hope and made him feel less friendless and alone.

"I missed you too, girl. I missed you too," he crooned into her neck. "It's time for us to find a way out of this place. I wish we could find Sydney." Dogma woofed again when Jordan mentioned Sydney's name.

"Yeah, I miss her too. Unfortunately looking for Syd would be like searching for the proverbial needle in a haystack. She could be anywhere. I think we should try to release the boys in the mines first."

Jordan sat on his bed. "We're at a disadvantage, girl. There's only two of us and nearly fifty of them. But they are used to following orders so maybe we can use that. Food is going to be my biggest problem. Again." He sighed. "We'll simply have to do what we can. No way am I sticking around this place to be Stud of the Year."

He lay back on the bed and pulled Dogma up next to him. It felt nice to have a companion again. He fell asleep and dreamt that Sydney lay curled up tight against him.

11

A WEEK HAD PASSED since Sydney's discovery of her father. She visited with him daily while on her walk, telling him stories of their life together in hopes of breaking loose his memory. Although he listened politely and seemed to enjoy hearing the family stories, he gave no indication that anything sounded familiar to him. At his request she stopped calling him 'Daddy' and began to address him as Alex.

Sydney began to accept that her father's amnesia was a permanent condition when Medicine Woman told her that he was unlikely to recover any more memories after such a long period of time. It was hard for Sydney to know how to behave with him; he was someone near and dear to her heart, and yet at the same time he was a total stranger. She wanted to hug him and touch him but couldn't do either without making him feel awkward.

The situation became easier when she discovered that he was fundamentally the same man that he had been before the accident robbed his memories. The *new* Alex--she couldn't help but think of him that way–loved the outdoors and the natural world as deeply as the old Alex had. He seemed to remember most of what he had learned as a biologist and was eager to share his knowledge with her.

As Sydney's strength grew her father took her on short hiking trips out into the desert plain and up into the mountains. She stopped telling him stories of the family he had lost and focused on their growing friendship instead. She found him easy to be with once she stopped nagging him to remember. They talked and laughed together, observed and appreciated the resiliency of nature.

He taught her how to set snares for small game and how to dig a pit trap that was shaped wider at the bottom so the prey couldn't climb out. He showed her how to work small arrow points for her crossbow bolts from flint, and how to make flint scrapers and knives.

She asked him where he had learned the skills he taught her and he told her that Medicine Woman's people had found him wandering in the mountains and had taken him in.

"Where are Medicine Woman's people?" asked Sydney. "Why aren't you and Medicine Woman with them?"

Alex looked uncomfortable. "The others moved to the west side of the mountains to their winter camp. There is an elk herd that winters there. Food is easier to hunt."

He hesitated, then placed his hand on her arm. "We couldn't risk moving you," he said. "You wouldn't have survived the journey over the mountains."

"You stayed behind for me? But…that means you're stuck here for the winter. You can't cross the mountains once the snows get deep." Sydney felt horrified by the sacrifice Medicine Woman and her father had made for her. "What if someone needs Medicine Woman's help?"

Her father shrugged. "She felt it was more important to help the person who needed her then. Medicine Woman is not a woman who dwells on what-ifs. We'll be fine here. I can provide for the three of us and we'll catch up with the others come spring."

Sydney knew Medicine Woman should be with her people. Winter was a bad time to be without a healer. She also felt grateful that the old woman had chosen to stay behind and save Sydney's life, especially now that she had her father back.

She looked at the man who had once carried her upon his shoulders and neighed like a horse when she demanded pony rides. Alex Waters had been a first class father, loving, kind, firm when needed, fun, and most of all, deeply committed to his family.

Sydney swallowed against the sudden lump in her throat. She still hadn't told her father about Shannon; how she had died while Sydney watched. How Sydney had acted the coward and kept hidden in the barn loft while…she shook her head, trying to dislodge the memories.

"What?" asked her father. He was watching her with a puzzled look on his face. "Medicine Woman doesn't regret her decision to remain behind with you, I can assure you of that."

Sydney turned her head so her father wouldn't see the tears hanging in her eyes. He didn't know. Should she tell him about Shannon?

He needs to know what kind of daughter I really am. But then he might want nothing further to do with her and she couldn't bear that.

She dashed the tears away before they could fall. "I owe you both my life. I'll never be able to repay you, but I'll do my best."

Oh, what a coward she was.

The weight in Sydney's chest grew heavier.

12

"Master James, the High Priestess would like to see you."

"Now?" Jordan and Dogma had just returned from their morning walk to the falls. The light snow that had fallen the previous day worried him. He had had no success trying to formulate an escape plan and the snow reminded him that time was growing short.

"Yes, now. Do you have something better to do?" The acolyte sounded taken aback that Jordan would even question a summons from the temple ruler.

"No, only, I just returned from my morning walk a few minutes ago and I'd like to warm up a bit first. The air is quite brisk you know." He tried flashing a smile at the acolyte.

"Oh. I'm sorry," she actually sounded sorry, "but I have orders to bring you to the High Priestess immediately. She'll be angry with me if I don't carry out her orders."

The girl sounded anxious. Jordan didn't want to see Mallory right this moment, but he didn't want to get the girl in trouble either. He told Dogma to stay and followed the girl.

Every other time he'd had an audience with Mallory it had been held in the large meeting room where he'd been brought the first time he met her. Today the acolyte surprised him when she turned in the opposite direction.

"Where are we going?" he asked. He focused on memorizing the turns they took in case he needed to find his way back here on his own one day.

"The High Priestess is in her private chambers. It is an honor to see them. Most of us have not been invited inside." She stopped and spoke to someone else. "I am delivering Master James to the High Priestess."

"He may enter. You must wait out here," replied a stern voice. "This way, Master James."

Jordan heard a doorknob turn, felt the air move past his face, and a hand gently pushed him into the room. The door closed behind him. He saw Mallory's aura stretched horizontal. Was she lying on a couch or a bed?

Nerves shivered down his back but he gave no indication that he saw her. His ability to see auras was his secret; let her believe he was completely blind.

The aura rose and moved closer to him. "Well, Master James. It is a pity you cannot see, my chambers are quite luxurious and I am very proud of them." She placed her hand upon his arm and gently guided him to a chair. "Have a seat, please. It is time we had a talk."

Soft carpets cushioned his steps. Jordan felt for the chair seat and lowered himself into it. He ran his hands over the soft leather. The chair was large and comfortable, built for a man. He wondered how many men before him had sat in this very spot. The smell of sandalwood hung heavy in the air. Incense? The chair and the sandalwood increased his nervousness. Why had she summoned him to her chambers?

"What would you like to talk about, Miss Dunne?" He was

proud of his feigned nonchalance, especially as his pulse was racing. He was afraid, afraid that now he was going to learn why the High Priestess was feeding and housing a blind man.

Man up, he told himself sternly. *You already know her plan.*

Mallory didn't speak right away. He heard her sip a liquid and set the glass on a table. He knew the table was made from wood; wood sounded different from glass which sounded different from slate or marble or plastic. His sister used to test him with sounds to help him feel more comfortable in unfamiliar surroundings.

He also smelled wine underneath the sandalwood. *So, the High Priestess likes her wine.* He filed the information away. It might prove useful later on. Mallory's next words surprised him.

"Do you know what drives the world's civilizations, Master James?" Her soft voice belied the intensity behind her question.

Jordan frowned. What was she looking for?

"Not really," he answered cautiously. "I guess I'd have to say religion and the pursuit of God."

"That's true, religion is a powerful motivator and one I employ myself, but you'd be wrong. The quest for riches is man's most powerful motivator, Jordan. Woman's as well. I may call you Jordan, mayn't I?"

She didn't wait for Jordan to answer. "And the most sought after riches is gold. Throughout man's history civilizations have been built and destroyed because of gold."

"Is gold important to you as well, Miss Dunne? I thought the Temple of Gaia was dedicated to honoring the Earth Mother."

Mallory laughed, a throaty, pleasant sound that should have charmed him, but instead made the hairs on the back of Jordan's neck stand up.

"Ah, Jordan, I believe you are sharper than you let on. Yes, gold is very important to me. My many-great granddaddy staked a claim on several mines in this area back when the first gold rush started in the west. He did well for himself and amassed quite a fortune. The Dunnes became leaders in the state and mixed with politicians and other wealthy families. We were an important family back then."

"I'm sure mining isn't easy," said Jordan. "Especially back then. You must be very proud of him." *Why was she telling him this?*

"Unfortunately his descendants were not as enterprising as Thaddeus Dunne and they soon spent the family fortune." Mallory sounded bitter and angry. "My mother grew up in the poor section of Fort Collins. She was fifteen when she had me, eighteen when she ran off with some loser. My grandmother raised me as best she could but she wasn't very intelligent. There were days we had nothing to eat. When I became old enough to work I promised myself I wouldn't be poor forever."

"I'm sorry, Mallory. That must have been awful for you," said Jordan softly. Mallory was so caught up in her story that she didn't notice he had used her first name. Her aura rose and began to pace the room.

"I worked as a programmer for a software company until I learned enough to strike out on my own. I started a small company, sold it to a bigger one, and used the money to buy back one of Thaddeus Dunne's mines. Everyone figured the mines were played out and no one valued them anymore so I picked up the land cheap."

"That was very clever of you. Do you own just the one mine?" Jordan couldn't believe she was telling him about her mines.

"Of course it was clever of me." Mallory's sharp tone told

Jordan she was glaring at him. He put an appropriately impressed expression on his face. It seemed to work as her tone softened.

"I'm smarter than most people. There are thousands of abandoned mines across the American West just waiting to be found and reworked. My plan was to buy up all the land that once belonged to the Dunne family, but the upheaval made that unnecessary. I simply moved into this resort, which sits on what was once Dunne land, and started the temple. The temple is important; it attracts the people I need to carry out my plan."

She gave a short laugh. "Most people are looking for a leader, you see. They don't want to be responsible for their own lives. People are basically sheep, Master James, just waiting to be led by the nose. They want someone else to tell them what to do and how to live and I am that person."

Mallory Dunne was one scary lady with a deeply warped view of the world. He needed to watch his step with her, he reminded himself.

"And what is your grand plan, Miss Dunne?" Jordan forced warm interest into his voice. "Once you've opened all these other abandoned mines, I mean."

Mallory's aura stopped in front of Jordan and leaned into him. She smelled of roses and wine, he noticed. He wondered where the wine came from. Perhaps the resort had boasted a wine cellar that had been left behind when the owners abandoned the place.

"Why, I intend to become the new leader of what's left of civilization, Master James. Gold is power, and I want power. This temple is only the beginning. I am going to attract the great masses of sheep who are wandering the country looking for someone to follow."

She took Jordan's hand and pulled him up from the chair. "Come with me. I'm going to show you something."

She led Jordan across the room and released his hand. He heard metal on metal and tumblers sliding until they clicked into place, then felt the air pressure change as Mallory pushed open a door. She reclaimed Jordan's hand and tugged him through the door into a cold room. He looked around the room and sensed piles of solid objects but saw no signs of anything living.

"Here, Master James, is what I have been working toward these last few years."

Jordan heard the reverence and excitement in her voice and knew that whatever was in this room, Mallory Dunne loved and admired it. Treasured it.

"I'm sorry I cannot appreciate what you are showing me," he said. "Would you be so kind and describe it to me?"

"Gold, Master James. You are looking at piles of gold. This room contains the gold from my ancestor's abandoned mines. The easy stuff had been stripped from the ground centuries ago, but I persevered and dug deeper, deep enough to uncover unsuspected pockets of the one element that every civilization covets."

Her voice had taken on a breathless quality, almost as if the gold excited her in a sexual manner.

She led him deeper into the room. "Did you know that a sheet of gold, one inch thick and twelve inches square, weighs close to one hundred pounds, Master James? Hold this." She turned up the palm of Jordan's free hand and placed a heavy object in it.

He freed his other hand from Mallory's grasp and felt the object. It was cold, about the size of a plum, odd-shaped and rough textured and surprisingly heavy for its size. "Is this a nugget of gold?" he asked.

"An especially fine specimen from my southern mine," replied Mallory.

"I'm sorry I cannot appreciate its color and shine." Jordan bit his tongue to keep from asking about the men's lives she squandered chasing her crazy dream.

Mallory chuckled and took the nugget from Jordan. "If you could see I would not be showing you this room. No one is allowed in here but me. Women are as greedy as men, Master James. Never forget that. Trust no one. I keep this room locked at all times and I have the only key."

He had to ask. He needed to hear the High Bitch confess her sin. "Who does your mining, Miss Dunne? Do the acolytes dig your gold for you.?"

Mallory didn't answer right away. She pulled Jordan from the room and relocked the door after him. After guiding him back to the chair she stood before him. He had the strong impression that something important was about to happen and he feared he wasn't ready for it.

Mallory picked up his right hand and began stroking it. Jordan resisted the urge to pull his hand back. He needed information and this was the person who knew what he needed to know. Her fingers felt smooth and cool against his skin. Alien.

"That's a very good question, Master James. Finding labor to work in the mines is a serious issue. No, my acolytes do not work in the mines, they are women and I try to protect women. I don't trust any of them, but I protect them. The acolytes serve another purpose for me, one you will soon learn about."

She stopped stroking and brought Jordan's hand to her face and pressed his palm against her cheek. "I send the men we find into the mines," she said, her voice a soft whisper against his skin. "As they have no lives they are grateful for the work I give them."

Somehow Jordan doubted that. A spark of anger ignited deep within him. It was clear that Mallory lived in her own made-up world. Before he could decide what to ask next, Mallory took his palm from her cheek and ran it down her neck and over her breast to her waist. She pressed his hand against her body and pushed it lower to her thigh.

Jordan felt the curve of her breast, the indent of her waist, and the swell of her hip. He snatched his hand away as she pushed it between her legs. It took all of his self-control not to wipe his palm on his pants.

Mallory chuckled, a low seductive sound. "Really, Master James. Are you that shy? In three weeks you will fill an important role for the temple. I need to know that you are capable." She took a step closer so her thighs pressed against his legs and leaned over him. Her lips brushed his ear. She took his earlobe between her teeth and bit it lightly.

He shuddered in response. His skin felt clammy, hot and cold at the same time.

"We need a man, Jordan, a strong and virile man to perform the most natural of acts between a man and a woman. This year you are that man."

Jordan jerked his head back. "No!" He felt beads of sweat pop out on his forehead. *Oh my god, she was trying to seduce him!* He hadn't expected this from Mallory. He thought a High Priestess would keep herself pure, would hold herself above the other women in the temple. Instead Mallory revealed a wanton side to her nature that increased Jordan's nervousness in a way her craziness had not.

Mallory wrapped her hand around the back of Jordan's head and pulled his face close to her own. "Yes," she said as she brushed her lips against his mouth. "You are a fine specimen and will bring new blood into my breeding program."

He cast about for a way to dissuade her. "You can't be serious. Why me? I'm imperfect—blind, remember?—and therefore of no use to you."

In response to his words Mallory sat on his lap and wrapped her arms around his neck. He had never held a woman on his lap. *Why hadn't he ever held Sydney in his lap before? He should have.* He felt the weight of Mallory's rounded hips and long thighs, the warmth of her breasts pressed against him. His abdomen clenched and he felt a little dizzy.

"I—I'm…blind. Bad for breeding."

Mallory pressed a finger against his lips. "Ah, but you were not born blind, were you? You told me that when I first interviewed you. You are perfect for us, Jordan."

His name sounded obscene on her lips. Jordan wished she would return to the more formal Master James.

"You will refuse no girl because she lacks perfect beauty, although I am proud to say that we only invite the attractive ones to live in the temple."

She removed her finger and ran her tongue over Jordan's lips, pushing one hand through the opening of his robe. "The girls are looking forward to their week with such a handsome young man," she said, her voice low and throaty.

The touch of her fingers on Jordan's bare chest felt like an electric shock. Her rose scent became thick and cloying and clogged his head. Her mouth tasted of red wine.

He could hardly breath. His pulse raced. Jordan knew that he was going to have a panic attack if he allowed her to sit on his lap one moment longer.

Enough! He wasn't a piece of meat or a performing monkey.

He stood abruptly and dumped the High Priestess on the floor.

Mallory squawked with anger and indignation and swore at him. Fortunately for Jordan a knock came on her door before she could punish him for rejecting her advances. And he knew without a doubt that she would punish him. He had the feeling no one dared reject or refuse the High Priestess. So be it. He did not want this woman. He didn't want any woman except for Sydney.

"I said I was not to be disturbed," she shouted at the intruder. There was a momentary silence at the door.

"Forgive me, Your Highness, but it's important," came the cautious reply.

Mallory swore again and walked to the door. Jordan remained standing in front of the chair. Could he leave Mallory's chambers while she was distracted? He took two steps toward the door and stopped. What was the point? Mallory would just have him brought back to her. He heard the door open.

"We have a problem," said the person standing in the hall. "One of the new recruits has escaped the northern mine."

"And you bother me with this now? He'll be dead within a couple days. The city boys have no clue how to survive in the mountains."

Although the two women whispered Jordan could hear them clearly. His hearing was better than most people's and Mallory and the stranger were not that far away from where he stood. He turned his head away and pretended not to listen.

"This one is different," said the intruder. "He's from one of the northern tribes and knows his way around the mountains. According to our spy he told the others he would get help and return for them. Should we send out a search party?"

Mallory thought for a moment. "Move everyone from the northern mine to the western and southern mines. Split them between the two. Remove all sign of them from the abandoned mine. Let the boy bring help if he can. They'll find nothing and think he is making it up. Reward the spy, but be careful no one sees you. We don't want the others to learn his identity."

Mallory turned toward Jordan. "We'll continue our talk very soon, Master James. Right now I have pressing business that needs my attention. Sarah will escort you back to your room."

As Jordan walked past Mallory she reached out and ran her hand lightly up his arm and squeezed his bicep. "I always get first crack," she whispered.

Jordan suppressed a shudder. He didn't have to ask, he knew exactly what Mallory Dunne was telling him. She would be the first woman to breed with him. He pressed his lips together and bit back a retort. *He'd rather die.* He bowed his head and wished her a good day, feeling as if he had just escaped the executioner's noose.

Alone in his room later that night, Jordan thought about Mallory's obsession with gold and power, and how she was willing to take people's freedom and lives to get what she wanted. Although she claimed differently, she even used the women in the temple.

She was no better than a ruthless dictator or a fanatic cult leader. The Cult of Mallory, hiding behind the facade of a temple devoted to Mother Earth. The acolytes followed her without question, believing that she offered them a better life than the one she took them from.

Wasn't that the primary trick of a cult leader?

Perhaps for some, like Ruby, life at the temple *was* better. But he was willing to bet that most of the mothers hated giving up their sons, especially knowing they would never see them again, despite Mallory's lie that the young boys were being sent to a men's temple.

Mallory had spoken freely to him about her plans and her hoard of gold. That couldn't be good, he realized. Her openness about her fortune in gold and her plans for the future meant that she didn't plan to let Jordan live once he had performed the duty she had captured him for.

She couldn't risk him sharing that knowledge with someone from the outside world; especially the knowledge about the gold. If anyone learned about Mallory's hoard the temple would become a target for thieves and worse.

He needed to make his escape and it had to be very soon, preferably before Mallory called him back to her chambers. Time was rapidly running out.

Jordan paced his room and came to a decision. He had no choice; he had to leave the temple tonight. He knew that he was sentencing himself to an unpleasant death by leaving, but he preferred to face the unknown in the mountains than sex with twenty or more strangers followed by certain death here.

His mind made up, he sat down and began to plan.

1 3

AFTER THE EMOTIONAL talk with her father Sydney returned to Medicine Woman's tepee filled with self-loathing. She joined Medicine Woman by the fire and held her hands close to the flames to warm them, avoiding the elder woman's piercing gaze.

From the corner of her eye she saw Medicine Woman study her in the firelight. She lowered her face, trying to hide the guilt she knew was written there for the healer to clearly read.

"Heartache can kill as surely as disease or injury, Sydney. I can see that you carry a heavy burden. Someday you must let others help you ease the load."

Sydney nodded, unable to look up, afraid the compassion she would find in the other woman's eyes would loosen her tongue. After several minutes she took a deep breath and raised her face. She looked into Medicine Woman's wise eyes and realized she didn't need to tell her, the healer saw everything.

Medicine Woman studied Sydney's face, then gave a curt nod, as if she had made up her mind about something.

"You are an extraordinary young woman, Sydney. In the old days you would have a husband and family by now, but times are different. I have been waiting for an apprentice for several years. The usual way is to find a woman who has finished raising her family and is therefore free to devote herself to the village, but that has all changed. The upheaval has destroyed our way of life, yet the people still need a healer. If you are interested I would be honored to teach you the healing ways."

Sydney's face flushed with surprise and pleasure. "I am honored that you find me worthy of such a great responsibility. Thank you, yes! I would love to learn how to heal people." Even as she said the words she realized how right they felt. Perhaps in some small way healing others would help atone for letting her sister die.

Sydney had always assumed that she would follow in her father's footsteps and become a biologist, maybe even work for the Fish and Wildlife Service. To that end she had studied botany and animal science in school.

After the world changed that dream died and all her energy became focused on surviving. She hadn't been able to think of anything beyond staying alive one more day, and she had not dared to dream about her future.

For the first time since the upheaval, Sydney felt as if she had been given the opportunity to build a future beyond mere survival, a future that would give her life purpose and bring her personal satisfaction. A future that would give her a role she could be proud of in the new world.

That was reason enough to accept Medicine Woman's offer, but Sydney also owed the old healer her life. She felt obligated to give back to her savior, and training to help and someday replace Medicine Woman was the best way she could repay her.

"I can't wait to begin," Sydney said with a small smile.

Medicine Woman smiled back, then turned serious. "Good. We'll start right away. I will show you how to make my restorative broth first. It cures many common ills."

The two women set to work, wrinkled and veined brown hands guiding smooth olive-skinned ones, one dark head bent next to one silver-white.

Later that night as Sydney lay on her pallet and listened to an unusual east wind blow around the tepee, she thought about how life had a way of taking a person down unexpected paths. She prayed that she would prove to be a competent healer. She prayed that Shannon had forgiven her, and she prayed that Jordan was happy.

She had a new hole in her heart from losing Jordan to add to the ones she already carried from Pop's and Shannon's deaths. No matter how hard she tried to push Jordan from her mind she thought of him daily. She wondered where he was and what he was doing. She wondered if he ever thought of her. Most of all, she wondered why he had left her without telling her he needed to leave.

Her father left the next morning for the mountains. He wanted to trap a bear before they all disappeared into their winter dens and he had already delayed his hunt far later than usual.

Sydney knew she was the reason for the delay, but instead of feeling guilt, she felt a secret joy that her father cared about her enough to postpone an important hunt. She helped Medicine Woman prepare him a substantial breakfast and then sent him on his way with a shy hug and a smile.

Before he left, her father gave Sydney a chunk of creamy

white flint stone to practice working new arrow points, and he promised to bring back some special clay and moss for Medicine Woman that only grew in the mountains.

Sydney continued with her training before her father had even disappeared from sight. Medicine Woman introduced her to the various herbs, roots, barks, and minerals that she employed in her healing work. Some were stored in pieces of birch bark that had been cut thin and folded into a clever envelope-like container. Powders were stored in empty, cured animal stomachs or intestines, or in small sacks made from thin tanned hides.

Every ingredient had more than one property and Medicine Woman patiently acquainted Sydney with each of them. They explored one at a time, observing with their eyes, smelling, feeling, sometimes tasting, sometimes making a thick ointment with bear fat and applying it to Sydney's wrist, sometimes inhaling the smoke in a special carved pipe that Medicine Woman kept wrapped in a piece of soft deerskin.

She learned that every part of a plant held a different medicinal property and was used for different ailments. Roots were considered especially potent as they held the life force of a plant, and plants with multiple roots were especially prized. These plants were usually gathered in the fall, when they had reached the state of full maturity, with the exception of early spring shoots needed to create spring tonics to shake off the effects of long, wearing winters.

By the end of the fourth day Sydney began to feel like a walking pharmacopeia. She could identify the various dried leaves and ground roots and powders by their distinctive smells.

Some plants were used for opposite ailments, which confused her, but Medicine Woman laughed and told her not to worry, she would soon develop a feel for the subtleties of healing. She explained that much of the healing art was intuitive and Sydney would eventually learn to listen to her inner self.

Late on the fourth night Sydney woke to the howl of wolves. Their long drawn out howls were nothing like the strange jarring yips of the coyotes that had lived around Sydney's home in Iowa.

The wolf's call sounded deeper, louder, stronger, and mournful. It sent icy shivers down Sydney's back in a way the coyotes call never had.

She sat up and found Medicine Woman awake and sitting by the fire.

Medicine Woman saw Sydney shudder. "They are hunting something, chasing it toward us. In all the years I've summered here I've never heard them this close. They usually hunt in the mountain forest. But I have never stayed here this late in the season, perhaps it is normal for them to hunt the plain this time of year."

She added several sticks of wood to the fire. "They should not bother us inside the tepee."

Sydney gave her a tremulous smile and straightened her shoulders, but she couldn't return to sleep. She moved closer to the fire and sat. She hated to admit to cowardice, but the wolves worried her. There was only a stiff buffalo hide covering the tepee's entrance; it didn't seem like much of a deterrent to a hungry hunter.

She focused on their calls as she gazed into the flames. Eventually Sydney began to detect a difference in their voices and thought she could identify five different wolves. She concentrated so intently on the variances in their calls that it took her a while to realize they were drawing closer to the tepee. She cast an anxious glance at Medicine Woman who sat expressionless, gazing into the fire.

Sydney crept to her pallet and grabbed her crossbow and half a dozen arrows. The flint points were only an inch long, more suited to small game such as rabbits and squirrels, but she hoped they would deter a wolf attack. She returned to the fire with the crossbow on her lap and focused on the calls again.

The wolves continued to draw closer.

To Sydney's ear their calls sounded wilder and more excited. They were closing in on their prey. She could almost picture their progress in her mind's eye. As they drew even closer to the tepee, Sydney glanced nervously at Medicine Woman but the old healer still seemed relaxed and untroubled.

Sydney couldn't stand the suspense any longer, she needed to know exactly where the wolves were and what they chased. She untied one set of the leather laces that held the flap closed at night and pushed it aside, wide enough to poke her head through.

The night air was crisp and cold, the black sky filled with stars and a waxing moon. The shallow coat of snow on the desert plain shone silver gray in the soft moonlight. Dark gray clumps of sagebrush and mesquite trees dotted the wide valley.

A nearby scream pierced the air. Sydney's heart leapt into her throat and a shiver convulsed her body. The wolves had closed in on their prey.

She heard nothing more for several seconds, then a shape burst around the side of the tepee and dove straight at Sydney. A jumble of wolves followed close on its heels.

"Get out of the way!" gasped a male voice, and pushed Sydney back into the tepee. He landed on top of her, then turned and kicked at a wolf that had stuck its head through the flap.

Trembling with fear, Sydney pushed herself free and scrambled to her feet. Ignoring the man who had brought the wolves to their door, she looked about the tepee.

Where was her crossbow? Not seeing it, she pulled a firebrand from the fire and shoved it at the wolf's face. It snarled and backed away. Sydney jabbed at the wolf again, then pulled the buffalo flap closed and quickly retied the laces.

The flap wouldn't keep the wolves out for long. She needed a better weapon, or a brilliant idea.

She recalled a story her father had told her about an old trapper he had traveled with for a while, a trapper who had survived a wolf attack. She handed the firebrand to their unannounced guest and darted across the tent.

"Fat, where's the bear fat?" she asked Medicine Woman. Sydney had experienced real fear before—when Shannon was murdered, as a prisoner in Jordan's storm cellar, when the killer Sir Thomas had held her at knifepoint—but those experiences paled beside the kind of fear she felt right now, the fear of being ripped apart alive by a hungry wild animal.

Medicine Woman pointed to the large badger hide bag that she used to store the fat. The healer used the fat to mix with some of her potions and always kept a supply on hand. They had been working with it just that morning, so it lay on top of the pile of hide bags.

Sydney scooped a handful of the soft, ivory-colored fat from its bag and grabbed the waste flint chips that she had neatly gathered for later removal. She pressed the sharp chips into several balls of fat, then returned to the door flap.

She could hear the wolves whining as they dug at the base of the tepee, looking for a way to get at the prey they had trapped inside.

The cries of the hungry wolves filled Sydney with fresh terror. She faltered for a moment then took a deep breath, untied the fasteners and edged the flap aside an inch at a time, until she had an opening wide enough to push her arm through. She tossed the bear fat balls as far from the tepee as she could.

A wolf leaped at the flap and momentarily trapped her arm. She felt its breath on her hand as its teeth scraped against her fingers. She tugged her arm back inside and retied the flap closed, hoping that the tale the old trapper told her father was true.

"Please work, please work," she prayed aloud. According to the trapper, the sharp-edged flint scraps would cut the wolf's mouth. The other wolves would smell the fresh blood and go after their injured pack member.

A few moments later she heard sharp cries followed by snarls. At least one wolf had taken the bear fat.

The remaining wolves abandoned the tepee and the human prey hiding within to go after their bleeding comrade. Sydney let out a cry of relief and fell to her knees.

"Oh god, it worked. It worked," she half-laughed, half-sobbed as she crossed her arms over her chest and hugged herself. Outside the tepee the terrible sounds of a brutal death grew louder and then quieted to an occasional snarl.

Sydney wiped tears of relief and fear from her cheeks and turned to face their unexpected guest. He stared at her with wide eyes, the firebrand still in his hand. She could see the moment he realized he was safe and the fear and adrenaline began to drain from his body. The hand holding the firebrand began to shake and he hastily placed the burning wood back on the fire.

"That was quick thinking," he said, straightening back up.

"Thank you. You saved my life. How did you ever think of a clever trick like that?"

"My father told me about it. Are you hurt? What's your name?"

The stranger was younger than her, Sydney realized as she looked at his face, but not by many years. She guessed him to be in his late teens or early twenties. He stood several inches taller than her and was slim to the point of emaciated. He wore his long black hair tied back in a ponytail, and his eyes were a brown so dark they seemed to glitter black over his sculpted cheekbones. His tattered jeans and sweatshirt were caked with dirt.

Instead of answering Sydney's questions, the stranger turned to Medicine Woman and bowed his head. "Grandmother, it is good to see you again. I thought you would have left with the others and I was hallucinating when I saw your tepee. I was sure I must be dying, leaving my body before the pain of being ripped apart by the wolves became too much to bear. I am very happy to find that I am still alive."

Sydney looked at him more closely, searching for a resemblance to the woman who had saved her life. "Medicine Woman is your grandmother?"

"Great-grandmother, to be precise, but that is too much to say. All the younger members of our village call her Grandmother."

Medicine Woman smiled at the young man. "It is good to see you alive as well, Daniel. Sit here and let me look at your wound." She patted the hide by her side.

Daniel sat as instructed. "They caught up with me outside the tepee and one of them grabbed my leg. I was lucky to shake him off."

Sydney saw that the lower right leg of his jeans was soaked in blood. Daniel took his knife and slit the leg of his pants to the knee so his grandmother could more easily treat the wound. His calf was bruised and the flesh torn and bleeding.

"Let me help." Sydney set a pot of water on the hot coals to heat and filled a bowl with the meat broth that Medicine Woman kept on the fire at all times. She handed the bowl to Daniel and he accepted it with a heartfelt thank you.

It took him all of thirty seconds to empty the contents. Wordlessly he handed it back to Sydney and she refilled it two more times before he told her he'd had enough.

While Medicine Woman cleaned the bite on Daniel's leg she answered his questions about the well-being of the other members of their village. He studied Sydney when Medicine Woman told him how she had been found near death and brought to the tepee to see if she could be saved.

Daniel winced as his grandmother prodded the wound. "John is a good and able man. I'm surprised he is not here with you now." He raised an eyebrow at his grandmother. "He should not have left the two of you alone."

"John's name is Alex," interrupted Sydney, "Alex Waters. Not John. He is my father, although he can't remember anything about his life before the head injury. He didn't just leave us, he went into the mountains to trap a bear for Medicine Woman at her request. She needed a new supply of fat and wanted the meat and hide. We expect him back any day."

Sydney felt compelled to defend her father's absence even though she knew Daniel was right to voice his concern for his great-grandmother.

Daniel searched Sydney's face. "Yes, you have his eyes. It is good that he found you alive. Ouch. Easy, Grandmother. You hurt my leg more than the wolf."

Medicine Woman ignored him and kept poking at

Daniel's leg. Sydney knew she was looking for any foreign matter that might have found its way into the wound.

"I need Jo. . . Alex's help," Daniel said when she stopped. "When he returns we must go back to the mines and free the other men. They gave me their food to help me build my strength, and then they covered for me so I could escape. They hid me in a side tunnel and pretended I had already escaped. When the High Priestess ordered the men moved to the other mines they left the mine unguarded and I was able to sneak away. I must return to them. I promised I would bring help. They will all die before their time if I do not. No one leaves those mines alive."

"Who is the High Priestess?" asked Sydney.

Daniel shook his head and stretched his wounded leg by the fire. Medicine Woman asked Sydney to make up the healing poultice for open wounds and watched carefully as Sydney went about gathering the necessary ingredients.

"She is an evil woman, that is all I know," replied Daniel. "I never heard her name, only that she heads a cult and calls herself the High Priestess. She has three abandoned gold mines and a large resort complex where she houses the cult's women. She named the resort The Temple of Gaia. Somehow she convinces the women and girls in her cult that they are doing something good for the planet. She also sends out bands of women to scour the countryside for men and boys to work in her mines."

He shrugged one shoulder and looked chagrined at his great-grandmother's pointed look. "What can I say, Grandmother? They caught me napping one afternoon and made me their prisoner. I had traveled many days without rest trying to get back here before the village left, and they found me sound asleep. They took me to the complex and showed me to the Priestess, and she told them to deliver me to the north mine."

Sydney's hands stilled and her breath caught in her throat. Was it possible that some of the cult's women had found Jordan the very same way? She had left him sleeping alone at their campsite while she hunted for their dinner. If Jordan had been captured it would explain why he had left without telling her first.

A tiny kernel of hope that she might see her friend again lodged in her chest. She handed Medicine Woman the prepared poultice and waited for her approval.

Medicine Woman sniffed at the crushed leaves and poked a finger into the fat. She nodded her approval. "Very good, Sydney. You have learned much. I am pleased."

"Do you…did you hear anything about a blind man at the complex or in the other mines?" asked Sydney. She watched closely as Medicine Woman applied the poultice to the cleaned wound.

The kernel of hope in her chest blossomed when Daniel nodded. "I heard some of the younger women talking about him as they led me through the building. They were saying that his blindness didn't matter because it wasn't a birth defect."

He shrugged his shoulders again. "Whatever that means."

"Jordan wasn't born blind, he lost his sight as a young boy in an automobile accident," Sydney answered, puzzled. Why would the circumstances of Jordan's affliction matter?

"Did you hear anything else? Did the High Priestess send him to one of the mines?"

Daniel shook his head no. "I don't think so. A blind man cannot find or dig gold. The only other thing I heard was that they are planning a week long celebration for the winter solstice, and this year's solstice is going to be extra special because it takes place over the full moon. The younger girls were quite excited about it."

Medicine Woman placed a folded bandage over the poultice and wrapped another around Daniel's calf to hold it in place. "I've cleaned the bite and applied Sydney's poultice," she said. "Animal bites are loaded with bacteria. It is important to keep watch for sign of infection. If it feels warm or reddens we must change our approach."

She stood and pulled two hides each from her and Sydney's pallets and placed them near the fire. "You will sleep here with us."

Daniel thanked both women, crawled onto the hides and rolled up inside the top one. He fell asleep within moments and began to snore softly.

"Will Daniel be okay, Medicine Woman?" asked Sydney as she looked down at his sleeping form. He looked younger, less worn and less anxious now that he slept. "I'm so thankful he made it here before the wolves got him. It was a near thing."

Sydney looked over at the older woman and wondered how to tell her she would have to leave with Daniel to find Jordan.

"Yes, it was a near thing," Medicine Woman agreed, "and it is not finished. When your father returns the three of you will have to go and rescue the others. There will be no time to cross the mountains to gather more men. The moon will be full in ten days. I have a feeling you will need to find your friend before the ceremony if you want to save him."

14

ONCE HE HAD MADE the decision to escape Jordan felt both relief and nervous tension. He set about his preparations without further delay. The day had been chilly with a brisk north wind; he expected it to be much colder once the sun set. He located his thermal underwear, stripped off his jeans and shirt, and put on the underwear, then redressed.

He pulled his few remaining clothes from the small dresser next to his bed and stuffed them into his backpack. Dogma followed him around the room while he worked, as if she knew something was up and she didn't want to miss out on whatever Jordan was doing.

His clothes, his staff, Dogma. Was that everything he owned? Jordan sat on the bed and ran his hand over the heavy wool blanket that topped it. The blanket reminded him that Mallory's followers had taken his sleeping gear when they placed him in this room and never returned it.

He stood and stripped the blanket from the bed and carefully folded it into thirds, then rolled it into a cylinder and tried to stuff it into the pack. There wasn't enough room. He felt the surface of the pack and found buckles and D-rings but no straps other than the ones he used to carry it on his back. He couldn't carry the blanket in his hands; he needed one hand for his staff and one hand for Dogma. That left no hands for the blanket.

He couldn't leave it. He knew that the blanket could mean the difference between making it through a cold night or freezing to death. He needed to find a means to tie it to his pack. Jordan pulled the sheet from the bed and tried to tear off a strip. The weave was too tight and the sheet refused to rip. He tried using his teeth to bite through the cloth with no better results. Frustrated, he flung the sheet on the bed. He needed to find a sharp edge to poke a hole in the sheet.

He went to the door of his room and listened. He heard the low murmur of female voices. His guard and someone passing down the corridor.

Jordan placed his hands on the wall next to the door and ran them from where the door met the floor to as high as he could reach. He ran his fingers over the door hinges but they were rounded and smooth. He took a step to the right and repeated the floor to ceiling movement until he reached the first corner of the room.

An easy chair sat in this corner. He imagined there had also been a reading lamp at one time but the lamp had been removed at some point, whether before his arrival or after he didn't know, nor did he care, except that a broken lightbulb would have given him something to cut the sheet with.

He flipped the chair over and felt along the seat bottom. A thin fabric covered the inner workings of the chair. Jordan tore the fabric aside and felt the large coil springs that supported the seat. A screw secured one end of the spring to the wooden frame; the other end was tied with heavy twine to the surrounding springs.

He worked his fingers into the center of the spring and

pulled as hard as he could. The metal stretched in his hand but remained secured to the chair. Jordan realized that even if he was able to work the spring loose it wouldn't give him the sharp edge he needed. He left the chair sitting on its side and continued working his way around the room.

The third wall contained a window. He knew this because he liked to sleep with the window open. Before Sydney took him into her life he could go weeks without stepping outside his parent's farmhouse. Safe and familiar, it had been his prison, and his sister a well-intentioned, loving jailer.

Now he couldn't bear for a single day to pass without being outdoors.

He stood before the window and placed his palms against the cold, smooth glass. Glass. Never in his life had he intentionally broken something made of glass, but glass would give him the sharp edge he needed. Broken glass was dangerous, but especially dangerous for a blind man. If he cut himself he would be unable to doctor his wound and would likely die of infection.

Just like his sister Torrie had.

Jordan pushed the fears from his mind. It had to be done.

Breaking the window would be noisy. He didn't want to alert his guard, not yet, not until he finished his preparations. Jordan made his way back to the bed and picked up his pillow. He stripped off the pillowcase, returned to the window and held the pillow against it, then punched the pillow. Nothing happened.

He punched it again harder and heard the window pane crack. One more hit and the pillow broke through.

Jordan stood and listened for several minutes but heard no activity outside his door. Apparently the pillow had muffled the sound of the breaking glass. He set the pillow on the floor and carefully walked his fingers across the window to the broken edge. He lightly grabbed one of the jagged edges and tried to pull it free from the window frame but it slipped from his fingers.

Jordan muttered a few choice swear words, then made his way back to his pack and dug out his leather gloves.

With his fingers protected the jagged glass piece was easy to wrestle free. He used it to slash the sheet, then tore the sheet into long, even strips. He set five strips aside, folded the remainder inside his rolled wool blanket and used two of the five to secure the blanket to his pack. He pulled the heavy drapes across the window to block the cold air rushing in the hole, afraid that the guard would feel the air flowing under the door.

Jordan stretched out on his stripped mattress and went over the rest of his plan. He wished his window wasn't so high off the ground as that would be the easiest way out. For all he knew it could be only six feet above the ground, but as he had no way to see for himself he had to believe Lorelei when she told him this second floor room faced the back of the building and the ground sloped away at a steep angle.

He would have to leave the building through the front door. After following Lorelei through the building twice a day for the last month or more, he knew exactly where the entry door was located. The trick would be getting the guard to unlock his door and getting her inside his room.

He patted the bed, inviting Dogma to join him, and pulled her close when she jumped up. Her presence gave him comfort and courage. He wasn't the only one who had changed since Sydney had come into his life. Dogma had learned a lot about survival and traveling through the wilderness. Jordan knew she would do her best to lead him and keep him safe.

Jordan dozed until the changing of the guard outside his

door woke him. He forced himself to wait a while longer to be sure the first guard had retired for the night. It wouldn't do to run into her in one of the hallways on his way out. The guards changed at midnight. The other acolytes should be in bed and sound asleep.

He crept to the door and listened but heard nothing. The day guard had left and the night guard was alone. It was time to put his plan into action. He grabbed his pack and set it behind the door so the guard wouldn't see it. He raised his fist to knock on the door but at the last second decided to open the drapes. The broken window would give him an element of surprise.

When all was set he rapped on his door. "Excuse me, Amy, are you there? I need help in here." Jordan stood back from the door and waited with the pillowcase in his hands. As he hoped, Amy entered the room and took a step toward the window. He quickly stepped behind the unsuspecting guard and pulled the case over her head, pinning her arms to her side.

"I'm terribly sorry to do this to you. Please don't take it personally. I like you well enough and I hope you don't get into trouble with Mallory, but I'm afraid I can't hang around here any longer." He grabbed one of the strips of sheet and wound it around the guard's face so she couldn't scream. "Can you breath?" Amy grunted and kicked at Jordan.

Jordan grabbed her and laid her on the carpet. "I don't want to be this year's sperm donor, you see," he explained as he wound the second sheet strip around the woman's torso and tied it off. "It has nothing to do with you ladies as I'm sure you're all very lovely. Stay still, please."

He wrapped the third strip around the guard's legs. "I'm sure most men would be flattered to be chosen for the honor, but I'm just not that kind of guy. I have someone, you see, someone I care for deeply, and if I can find her I'm going to ask her to marry me. So I really must leave."

He picked up the guard and placed her on the bed. She rolled off and fell to the floor with a soft thump and a muffled cry.

"That won't do. Someone might hear you." Jordan found his pack and pulled two more sheet strips from it and tied the guard to the bed frame. "There. Now you won't hurt yourself. Someone will set you free in the morning."

He picked up his pack and staff and stood in the open door listening. All was quiet. He closed and locked the door behind him then pocketed the key. If they had to hunt up a key it would buy him a little more time. He saw no auras as he and Dogma padded silently down the carpeted hall and down two flights of stairs.

He stopped and put his ear to the door at the bottom of the stairwell but heard nothing. The door made a loud whoosh as Jordan pulled it open. He grabbed Dogma's ruff to hold her back and listened again, relaxing a bit when he felt sure that the acolytes were all in their rooms.

He held the stairway door open for Dogma and followed her into the large foyer. His hesitated when he heard his footfalls echo as he crossed the tiled space but didn't stop. He reached the entry and slid back the large deadbolt on the heavy wooden door. He pulled it open only wide enough to squeeze through, then slipped out into the night, pulling the door closed softly behind him.

Jordan stood on the porch for a moment savoring the sense of freedom. How long ago was it that the six acolytes had found him and brought him to this porch and to Mallory Dunne? At least one month, he guessed. However long a period of time, it had been far too long. It was well past time for him to leave.

"Let's go, Dogma," he whispered. "Let's find Sydney. But first the mines. There are a lot of men who need our help."

Jordan headed for the waterfall. He identified the short, yellow-green glow of the meadow grasses and the taller, elongated auras of the forest trees beyond. He knew the way to the falls without Lorelei's guidance. He hoped that the falls would lead him to the woodcutters and Big Mike. He felt sure the woodcutters would help him get away from the temple and he hoped he could convince them to help free the miners.

Jordan was glad he had thought to put on his thermal underwear. The night air felt crisp and cold in his lungs and on his face. He wore his gloves and moved at a steady pace to keep warm. No breeze blew tonight and he could hear the falls in the quiet. Jordan followed the sound of the water until he stood on the edge of the pool beneath the falls.

"This is where I saw Big Mike, Dogma. He came from the other side of the stream, so that's where we need to go. He told me there's a bridge that crosses above the falls. Let's see if we can find it." Jordan turned to his left and followed the sound of the rushing water. The land beneath his feet jutted up abruptly and he released Dogma's ruff so he could keep one hand on the ground to feel his way.

He made his way to the top of the falls one careful step at a time with Dogma on his heels. A few times the ground became almost vertical and he was forced to crawl on his hands and knees. He took his time, made sure of every step as Sydney had taught him when moving over unfamiliar territory. He tested each branch that he grasped to help pull him along, each patch of ground before he put his full weight on a foot. A fall down the steep slope would surely mean a broken bone or worse.

The slow progress frustrated him. He needed to be well

away from the temple before anyone discovered his guard tied to his bed. Poor Amy. He hoped Mallory didn't punish her too badly for his escape. He wished there'd been another way to leave without making her look incompetent.

Jordan pushed Amy from his thoughts. He concentrated on putting one foot in front of the other and on keeping his forward progress going until finally he reached the top of the falls.

"Dogma, we need to find the bridge. It should be right here. Where is it girl?" Jordan stood and poked at the stream bank with his staff. He felt water and rocks. He took three steps and felt again. More water and rocks. On the third try his staff clunked against wood.

Jordan swung the staff in front of him. The way to the bridge seemed clear. He stepped forward and reached out with his toe to feel for the edge of the bridge. He felt a rounded log laid parallel to the stream's edge. With his staff in hand he stepped onto it and found another laid next to the first. The narrow bridge possessed no handrail. A slip off the downstream side would mean an unpleasant trip over the falls.

"Stay here, Dogma," he commanded. He needed to cross the bridge alone; it wasn't wide enough for them to cross together and he was afraid Dogma might accidentally push him off the side. Dogma whined but did as commanded. Jordan sent a silent prayer to Torrie, thanking her for the excellent training she had given the great beast before she died.

The bridge dipped and wobbled under his weight. He heard water slosh and hoped his boots were staying dry. He crossed the stream one log at a time, stopping on each one to check with his staff that he hadn't veered from the center of the bridge. Relief flooded through him when he stumbled off the bridge onto the far bank. He took a moment to breath deeply and calm his shaking hands.

Jordan called Dogma and then spun in a slow half-circle. The jumbled auras of the forest glowed a dull green. He searched for a break in the auras that would indicate a path into the forest. Big Mike must have been following a path when he'd found Jordan, he reasoned. There had to be one near the bridge.

He stepped away from the stream bank and saw it: a winding, narrow black space running through the soft green light.

"C'mon Dogma, let's see if we can find Big Mike and his friends." Dogma pressed against Jordan's thigh and they headed down the path, stopping on occasion to listen to the forest around them.

Jordan lost all sense of time and direction. The path climbed and dipped and climbed and dipped until he wasn't sure if he was on a mountain or in a mountain valley. He might have felt lost except that the path was well-worn and cleared of any brush. Somehow he knew that it was frequently used and that gave him hope that he would find either a mine or the woodcutter's cottage at the end of it.

When he stumbled into a clearing Jordan almost shouted for joy. His legs and feet ached and he felt so tired he thought he could sleep standing up. He smelled woodsmoke on the air and pumped his fist. This had to be the woodcutter's cottage.

He scanned the clearing until he found a large blank spot in the auras. He headed toward the spot knowing that it had to be the cottage.

The clearing was silent except for Jordan's steps in the dried leaves. He stopped and looked at what he assumed was the cottage. What if Big Mike thought he was a thief or something worse? He might attack Jordan first and ask questions later. Jordan decided the safest approach was to let Big Mike know he was there before he got too close.

"Mike! Mike Keene! Are you here?" he shouted. He felt Dogma tense against his leg and knew she'd heard someone inside the cottage. He called again. "Mike! It's Jordan, Jordan James from the temple. We met at the waterfall."

"Jordan? How on earth—?"

Jordan heard Mike's deep rumble and he laughed. "Yeah, it's me. Can we come in?" Relief washed over him. Big Mike was home, all would be well. Mike would help Jordan get the men out of the mines and maybe even help Jordan find Sydney.

"Who's we?" asked Big Mike, his voice wary.

"Me and Dogma, my dog. She helps me out. She's harmless, although I'm told she looks scary."

There was a minute of silence. "Just a minute, let me get some clothes on."

Jordan stood waiting. He wondered if the other woodcutters were awake. They must be, he thought, no one could sleep through all that shouting. He saw Big Mike's aura appear and approach him.

"Well, how 'bout that?" said Big Mike. "I never thought I'd see you here, Jordan. What are you doing up this way? And how on earth did you ever find me? I thought you were blind." His last statement sounded almost accusatory.

Jordan didn't feel comfortable telling Big Mike about his ability to see the auras of living things. That was a secret only Sydney knew about. "I took it slow and Dogma helped me. She picked up your trail. I was just hoping she was leading me the right way. For all I knew she could have been following a deer or a bear."

Mike seemed to accept his explanation. He clapped

Jordan on the shoulder with his big hand and invited him inside.

"I don't want to disturb your roommates, Mike. I can wait out here until they get up for work." Jordan had the distinct impression that he'd thrown Mike for a loop. The man sounded friendly enough but something felt a little off.

"Room—oh, yeah. Not to worry, son," said Mike. "They're off on the job. If the work is far enough away we sleep outside instead of traveling back to the cottage every night. Saves walking a lot of miles. Come on in. I'll heat you up some stew."

Jordan followed Mike into the cottage and sat on the chair Mike led him to. The cottage couldn't be much, he surmised. It had a hard packed dirt floor and smelled of woodsmoke, dirty socks, and meat stew. He detected a faint mustiness, like the smell of moist rotting wood, underneath the other odors.

"So Jordan, why are you here?" asked Mike again as he went about heating the stew.

The food smelled wonderful and Jordan's belly growled, reminding him that he'd missed two meals that day. He took a deep breath and wondered where to start his story.

"Mallory, uh, Mallory tried to seduce me today. And someone escaped from the north mine. I don't want to be Father of the Year to a bunch of children I'll never even meet. So I decided it was time for me to leave the temple. I was hoping you could help me get the men out of the other two mines."

Big Mike chuckled. "So, the High Bitch tried to seduce you, huh? She does like to get first crack at the men."

That's exactly what she said," said Jordan, thrown off balance for a moment. Mike set a bowl of stew on the table in front of Jordan. He inhaled the heavenly aroma of smoked ham and beans. Ham? "Smells wonderful. Where did you get ham, Mike?"

"Oh. I sneak some food from the temple occasionally. Never quite have enough you know. Tell me, what happened with Mallory?"

Jordan shrugged as he began to shovel stew into his mouth. "Fortunately she didn't get far," he said, after he'd taken several spoonfuls. "She showed me her storeroom of gold and then sat in my lap and I dumped her on the floor. Then an acolyte came to the door and told Mallory that someone had escaped from the north mine and she sent me back to my room. I decided it was time for me to leave and here I am."

Mike didn't say anything for several minutes while Jordan finished what he wanted of the bowl of hot stew. He set it on the floor and invited Dogma to lick the remainder clean.

"Mallory showed you her storeroom?" said Mike, sounding surprised and curious.

"Yeah, she said that since I can't see she felt safe showing all her gold to me. I had the sense that there was quite a bit in there. She gave me a nugget to hold. It was surprisingly heavy."

"Huh. So you were in Mallory's chambers and she showed you the gold and then tried to seduce you." Mike sounded thoughtful.

"She must have a suite of rooms or a connecting room because she unlocked the room with the gold and then locked it back up." Jordan didn't want to talk about Mallory and her crazy plans anymore.

"Do you know where the west and south mines are?" he asked. "Mallory told the acolyte to have everyone from the north mine moved to those two mines. I thought we could get the other woodcutters and find them."

"We can do that, Jordan, but it will have to wait until morning. Why don't you catch a few hours sleep and we'll head out after sunrise."

Big Mike settled Jordan on a bed of spruce branches that were piled on the floor opposite the wood stove. Jordan was almost asleep when he heard the cottage door open and softly close. He looked around the room but saw only Dogma's aura lying next to him.

Where had Mike gone? he wondered, then realized the big man probably needed to relieve himself outdoors as it was obvious there was no bathroom inside the cottage. He rolled over to face away from the door and fell asleep before Mike returned.

Jordan woke the next morning to the smell and sound of bacon sizzling, He quickly rolled his blanket and attached it to his pack, then shared his breakfast with Dogma who licked his fingers in gratitude. Big Mike had little to say and Jordan didn't interrupt his thoughts until they had left the woodcutter's cottage.

"Do you have a plan?" asked Jordan.

"Plan? For what?"

Big Mike seemed more distracted than a man on a rescue mission should act.

"For getting the miners out of the mines. How many guards are there? Do they guard only the mine entrance, or is there more than one entrance? Will we be able to sneak by them or will we have to confront them? I'm not sure how much help I'd be in a fight."

"Don't worry, I have it all worked out. I'll let you know what to do when we get there."

Jordan followed Big Mike in silence. It wasn't until the sun rose above the trees that he realized they were headed north. "Why are we going north? I thought the miners were moved to the south and west mines?" he asked, stopping.

"You can tell which way we're going?" asked Mike, surprised.

"I feel the sun on my face. I should feel it on my left cheek or the back of my head, but I feel it on my right cheek which means we're headed north," said Jordan. "Why?"

"There's an easier access trail from the north mine to the west mine. Otherwise we have to climb a steep mountain peak. This way is faster, trust me."

Big Mike resumed walking and Jordan followed. Who was he to question Mike? He knew absolutely nothing about these mountains. If Big Mike knew of an easier passage then they should take it and conserve their energy for the task ahead.

They walked another hour before Mike stopped. He waited for Jordan to draw alongside.

"We're here. I want to thank you for all the help you've given me, Jordan. Five years of waiting and scheming and it took a blind man to show me the way."

"What help? Of course I'm only too happy to—" Jordan's confused words were cut short when Big Mike shoved him hard. "Hey! What are you doing?"

Big Mike shoved him again, his large, meaty palms flat against Jordan's chest. Jordan flung out his arms and tried to catch his balance. He took a step back, then another. Mike shoved once more and Jordan felt only empty space beneath his feet.

Jordan clamped his mouth shut as his stomach seemed to slide inside his abdomen. The sensation of free falling was not one he enjoyed. It brought back the unpleasant memory of an occasion when his sister hadn't been there to look after him.

When he was sixteen he had given a performance for the Swedish king and queen. Afterwards their teenaged son took it upon himself to take Jordan out for some fun. That fun included a ride on a roller coaster, a terrifying experience for a blind boy who had no idea what a roller coaster ride entailed. He had been violently ill during and after the ride.

This fall lasted only seconds. Jordan landed on his back on a hard surface. The backpack drove the air from his lungs, leaving him stunned and gasping for breath. His lungs refused to pull in oxygen. They felt flattened, like a fallen soufflé, never to inflate again.

Jordan gasped and choked and heard strange "uh, uh, uh" noises that he realized were coming from him. At last the vacuum in his lungs broke and he strained to fill them. His heart pounded as he inhaled and exhaled loudly, desperate to replace the missing oxygen. Gradually his heartbeat slowed and his panic faded.

Once the trauma of having the wind knocked out of him receded Jordan realized he'd sustained other injuries in the fall. The back of his head hurt and his left wrist felt either broken or severely sprained.

When his breathing became normal again he slowly turned over onto his hands and knees. The pain in his head sent shudders through him and he threw up his breakfast. *Ah crap. Another head injury—just what I need.*

He took a deep breath and choked. Something big had died close by and the stench of rotting flesh made him retch again. The retching made his head pound and his wrist throb. Through his pain he heard Dogma snarling and snapping somewhere above him.

"Call off your dog. Jordan," yelled Mike. "You hear me? Call off your dog or I'll toss her down there too."

Without lifting his head Jordan called to Dogma. He

wanted answers from Mike, and he wouldn't get them as long as Dogma was attacking the woodcutter. He shifted his weight back onto his knees and held his swelling wrist with his uninjured hand.

"Who are you, Mike?" His voice sounded weak and he forced himself to speak louder. "Are you even a woodcutter or was everything you told me a lie?" Jordan's head throbbed with every word he spoke. He fought the urge to vomit again.

He released his wrist and lifted his hand to the back of his head and gingerly felt around. His hair was sticky with blood but his skull felt intact—not flattened or broken. He thanked his stubborn James ancestors for their thick skulls. He had a concussion but no brain injury. He could live with that.

"Where am I?" He laid back down to ease the pain in his wrist and the steady throb in his head. His injuries seemed worse when he sat upright. The ground felt hard and cold and damp under his cheek and the smell of the nasty dead creature filled his nostrils. He took shallow breaths through his mouth but it was impossible to avoid the stench of death.

"You're in a test shaft near the north mine," said Big Mike from overhead. "Sorry, Jordan, but you know how it is. Every man for himself these days. Nothing personal you know. I've been waiting to get my hands on Mallory's gold for years but until you came along no one knew where she hid it."

Mike didn't sound very sorry. He sounded positively jovial, in fact. Mike's cheerful attitude made him feel surly. "Well, bully for you, Mike. Why'd you have to push me into this hole?"

"Think about it, Jordan. I need time to steal as much gold as I can move. I can't take a chance that you'll show up at the temple with your rescued miners and get in my way. Even more important, without you alive to finger me Mallory will never know who robbed her and I won't have to worry about her sending anyone after me. I'll be able to make a nice clean getaway."

Mike sounded pompous and smug. He lowered his voice to a more intimate tone and continued. "Besides, with you out of the picture they'll be needing a man for their Solstice Ceremony and that's one chore I do enjoy. I'll set up my getaway, offer the ladies my services, and be on my way with enough gold to support me for the rest of my life."

Jordan's head pounded so loudly he could barely understand what Mike was saying, but he understood the important thing. Mike planned to leave him there to die. He lifted his head and spoke as loud as he could. "Best of luck to ya, Mike. Dogma, ATTACK."

He heard Mike scream as Dogma went for him. Jordan knew exactly what Dogma was doing to the traitorous woodcutter. His sister had explained the great beast's bloodlines and capabilities to him when she first brought the unusual puppy home.

One branch of Dogma's ancestors had belonged to the Nazi army. Hitler's dogs attacked the allied soldiers with a slash and run style that stymied his foes, harrying their victims until blood loss brought them down.

Jordan faded in and out of consciousness as the battle raged above. He barely registered the sound of Dogma's snarls and Big Mike's grunts as Mike tried to protect himself from the dog's sharp teeth. Eventually he heard crashing in the woods and knew that Big Mike had escaped.

Jordan tucked his injured wrist against his abdomen to immobilize it and curled into a ball. There was no hope of rescue. No one would come looking for him. He prayed that death would not take too long to claim him and then let the blissful peace of unconsciousness take him.

15

THREE DAYS PASSED BEFORE SYDNEY, her father, and Daniel were able to head south to the mines. Sydney had been anxious to leave the day after her father's arrival, but Medicine Woman refused to let Daniel travel until he had recovered from his recent ordeal. Daniel's grandmother insisted that he needed food and rest before facing the arduous journey back to the mines, and after Sydney's own near-death experience she couldn't argue with the elder woman.

Although she had no choice but to wait, Sydney's impatience grew daily, as did her fear for Jordan. What little information Daniel had learned about the cult of Gaia made her uneasy. Why would a cult made up of women wish to keep a blind man in their midst? It made no sense and it worried her.

She had read about cults in the past, and about cult leaders who led their followers to do unimaginable things. Cults that murdered innocent people, cults that took their own lives and those of their children, cults that sacrificed victims to obscure gods, or the sun, or the moon, or…Sydney shuddered. What if the all-female temple was planning to offer Jordan as a solstice sacrifice?

She forced herself to heed Smokey's advice to concentrate on the moment and on what she could affect. She couldn't help Jordan until she was with him and could assess the situation. There was no point in dwelling on what-ifs.

She was frustrated by another short delay when Daniel refused to leave Medicine Woman alone. The old woman told him not to be foolish, she could take care of herself and they wouldn't be away that long, but Daniel remained adamant about leaving his grandmother unprotected. They finally reached a compromise when Medicine Woman promised to spend the nights in Alex's cabin, a structure sturdy enough to keep out the wolves should they return.

Sydney felt ready to leap out of her skin with impatience by the time the trio set out. They each carried packs filled with the bare minimum of clothing and dried pemmican for the men they hoped to help.

Medicine Woman stuffed packets of medicines for the miners into Sydney's backpack and gave her last minute instructions on how to use the ones she hadn't studied yet.

"Trust in yourself, young one," said the old woman as they were leaving. "You know enough now to let your intuition guide you. If you have any question, hold the packet of medicine close to your abdomen with your right hand and touch the patient with your left hand. If it is the proper one to use the medicine packet will pull closer to your body. If it is wrong it will push away from you. The movement is very subtle so you must pay close attention. Just close close your eyes, breath evenly, and focus on whatever ill you are striving to help."

Medicine Woman grasped Sydney's arm and locked her dark eyes on Sydney's face. "I have faith in you, Sydney. You will do well. Be safe and take care of our menfolk. I'll await your return so we may continue your training."

Sydney gave Medicine Woman a quick hug, suddenly reluctant to leave the old woman alone. "Maybe I should stay here with you—"

Medicine Woman put two fingers on Sydney's lips to stop her words. "You must go. It is important for a healer to make this trip and I am too old. You will be needed, I have seen it in my dreams." She took her fingers away and smiled. "The men are waiting for you. Go now."

Sydney leaned down and impulsively kissed the woman on her dry, wrinkled cheek. "Thank you, Grandmother. Thank you for everything. We will return as quickly as possible." She hurried after her father and Daniel.

Daniel pushed them hard, anxious to keep his promise to the miners and return to his grandmother. The clouds piled up and turned the sky a solid, ominous gray. "Snow," was all Daniel said, and he pushed them harder.

They slept in short spurts and traveled through the nights. On the third night they stopped and made a real camp. The temperature had dropped and Sydney smelled snow in the air.

"We're almost there," Daniel said as he waited for Sydney to distribute the rabbit her father had snared and roasted over their first fire. The hot food tasted good after eating cold, dried venison meal after meal. The heat of the flames warmed Sydney's tired muscles and made her drowsy. She almost wept with joy when Daniel decided to spend the remainder of the night there in order to marshal their strength for the ordeal ahead.

Needing no further prompting, Sydney crawled into her sleeping bag and fell into a deep sleep, never waking until her father shook her awake before sunrise the following morning. They washed their pemmican down with hot herbal tea, broke camp, and were on their way before the first rays of the sun broke the eastern horizon.

Now that they were close Daniel increased their pace to a slow jog. Sydney stretched her legs to match the two men's longer steps. She felt strong and muscular and capable, better than she'd felt in years. The months of walking across the country had strengthened her legs and increased her endurance to a level she had never experienced before.

She pictured herself as her favorite heroine when she was a young girl, Wonder Woman. Wonder Woman had been a terrific role model, bold and ready to face any danger. The mental image of her own slim body dressed in the shapely super heroine's revealing costume brought a smile to her face.

The leafless trees made it easier to see into the forest around them, especially with the light blanket of snow on the ground. Deer tracks criss-crossed the mountainside. Daniel followed the worn animal trails, leaping fallen trees and rarely slowing. Chickadees flitted from branch to branch, following their progress with a cheerful "dee-dee-dee." Sydney could almost forget that they were on a rescue mission.

Small flakes of snow had begun to fall when Daniel stopped and pointed. "That's the trail to the north mine. No one's there now so we won't bother to check it. According to the miners, the closest mine to this spot is the west mine. We'll head there first." He started down a trail that looked as if it had been trampled by many feet.

"This trail looks well-traveled, Daniel," said Alex. "Is that from moving the miners or is it used by others?"

"I don't know," answered Daniel. "It looked like this when

I escaped the mine, but remember I left after the others did." He frowned. "Does it make a difference?"

Sydney's father gave a small shrug and pursed his lips. "It'd be nice to know if we're likely to run into someone, especially an unfriendly someone."

"I can't answer that, Alex," said Daniel. "I've never been to the other mines and the men I was imprisoned with were ignorant about them. There are the guards, but I don't know how many and I don't know if they travel between the mines. I saw only the one. Perhaps we should spread out on the trail; keep in sight of one another but not too close together. That way, if we do run into a guard it will be harder for him to capture all three of us."

Daniel headed down the trail with Alex thirty feet behind him. Sydney brought up the rear. She nocked an arrow in her bow and carried it in her hand. If a guard stopped her father or Daniel she could distract or injure him with a well-placed shot.

Fifteen minutes later she heard a whimper coming from her right. "Alex, wait a minute," she hissed. Her father kept walking. Sydney stooped and picked up a small rock and lobbed it at her father, hitting him in the back. He whirled around and she held up her palm and jerked her head in the direction of the noise.

"I heard something," she whispered.

Alex called softly to Daniel and the three of them stood and waited. After several minutes Sydney shook her head. "I guess I was mistaken."

She took a step forward. A long, anguished howl broke the silence and sent a shiver down her spine.

"It's just a wolf," she said, suddenly anxious.

Daniel held up his hand. "That was no wolf. It sounded more like a dog. We better check it out," he said quietly.

They left the trail and climbed through the trees, walking abreast and within sight of one another. Sydney stopped and cupped her ears with her hands. She heard the whimper again and veered off to her right.

After several minutes she broke into a small clearing. Dogma lay on her belly in the center of the clearing. She lifted her head and looked at Sydney, then leaped to her feet and ran to her with a joyous bark.

"Look out, Sydney!" Her father ran forward, then stopped short when he saw the dog put her front paws on Sydney's shoulders and lick her face. Sydney buried her face in the dog's neck.

"Huh, I assume you two know each other," he said with a smile.

Dogma responded by licking every part of Sydney she could reach, until Sydney giggled and hugged her close. "Dogma, I'm so happy to see you too, girl. How did you end up here? Where is Jordan?"

At the sound of Jordan's name Dogma dropped to the ground and trotted back to the spot where she had been lying. Sydney trailed behind her, stopping short when she saw the wide hole in the ground. She dropped her pack and carefully crept forward, testing the ground with each step.

When she neared the edge of the hole she dropped to her stomach and inched forward. Before she could see down into it the sickening stench of decay hit her in the face. She closed her eyes. *We're too late, Jordan's dead.*

Her heart pounded in her chest and tears squeezed out beneath her eyelids. Beside her, Dogma whined. She put out a shaking hand and rubbed the dog's ear.

"Is your friend down there?" her father asked.

Sydney's throat grew thick with tears. She could only nod, then crawled back from the edge of the hole. She couldn't bear to see Jordan's dead, decaying body. She wanted to remember him as the beautiful, vibrant man she had fallen in love with.

She sat ten feet away from the hole and called Dogma to her but the great beast refused to leave her master's body. *What kind of god killed a beautiful, peaceful man like Jordan James?*

Anger coursed through Sydney and mixed with her heartbreak. She watched through her tears as her father and Daniel approached the hole warily.

"There's a man and a dead deer down there," said Daniel quietly. He grabbed Alex's hand to secure himself and leaned farther out over the hole's edge. "One man, a deer carcass, and a backpack. I think the man may still be alive. Injured, but alive."

Alive? Sydney wiped the tears from her face with the back of her hand.

"Let me see!" She leaped to her feet and ran back to the hole. Her father grabbed her by the back of her pants as she leaned over the edge. She saw the deer carcass lying about twelve feet below. Jordan lay curled into a ball against the side of the hole, as far from the dead deer as he could get. As she watched, a shiver ran through him.

"He's alive!" whispered Sydney. "Jordan, it's me, Sydney."

Jordan didn't respond. Sydney tried again, slightly louder this time, still afraid to speak in normal tones or shout. Jordan still ignored her.

"He must be unconscious," she said to the others. "We have to get him out of there."

Jordan was dreaming of better times. In his dream he could see. He lay in a soft bed with Sydney's warm body tucked against his side. His beautiful Sydney, the girl who smelled of spice and fresh green plants. The girl who was now his wife and would never leave him.

The girl he loved more than life itself.

She whispered his name into his ear and he smiled and pulled her closer. Surely he was the luckiest man alive. She spoke his name again, a little louder this time and he frowned. There was no need to raise her voice in bed. Bed was the place for the soft intimacies of love. He tried to shush her but she ignored him and shouted his name.

Jordan swam up through the haze, fighting to bring back his dream. It was so much better than his current reality. His prison was filled with the stink of death and he was freezing cold and thirsty. He had already emptied his water bottle during one of his lucid spells. He had no idea how long ago that had been, no idea how long he had been trapped down in this hellhole.

"Jordan, listen to me," said Sydney's father. "We're going to get you out of there, just hang on, son."

Son. No one had called him son since the day his parent's car had been rammed by a drunk driver. Did this mean he was dead then? Had he finally joined his father and mother and sister? He opened his eyes and blinked. All he could see was a faint red-purple glow.

Jordan closed his eyes. Even in death he was blind. Bummer.

Sydney stood next to her father, his hand still on her back, and watched Jordan close his eyes. She knew about seeking the comfort of dreams to escape the reality of life. Only a short while ago she herself had hovered on the brink of death.

She grabbed her father's arm.

"Dad, we have to get him out of there." She didn't notice her slip of the tongue. It was natural for her to call this man Dad, he was her father even though he didn't remember his family.

Sydney looked across the hole to Daniel. "Do you have any ideas?" she asked.

"Maybe," said Daniel. He turned to Sydney's father.

"I passed a woodcutter's cottage when they first brought me here. They must have axes and rope there. The cottage isn't far, I'm going to see if I can locate it. In the meantime we'll need a travois to transport Sydney's friend once we get him out of the hole. Maybe you could work on that while I'm gone." He whirled away from the hole and ran off before Sydney or Alex could answer.

"What can I do to help?" asked Sydney.

Her father was already walking toward a grove of spruce on the clearing's edge. "Help me cut spruce boughs, the longer the better. Then we'll need some lengths of vine to tie the branches to the travois supports. I saw some Virginia Creeper growing up several oak trees not far back. We can use those."

Sydney took a moment to give Dogma water and some of her jerky, then joined her father and set to work. They soon amassed a large pile of spruce branches. Every few minutes Sydney walked to the edge of the hole and spoke quietly to Jordan, telling him to hang in there, rescue was on the way.

Jordan's lack of response worried her but she pushed it from her mind. If Medicine Woman could bring Sydney back from the edge of death surely she could help Jordan.

When her father decided they had enough boughs they descended to the trail they had been following earlier and backtracked to the vine-covered oaks. Sydney was amazed her father had noticed the creeper. It's bright red fall leaves were long gone and only a keen eye would have noticed the brown vines climbing the oak trunks.

The creeper was harder to harvest than she expected. It clung tight to the oak's rough bark with thousands of tiny roots, making it tough to get a handle on. Her father showed her how to dig the tip of her knife between the trunk and the vine and work a section loose large enough for Sydney to push her hand into.

Once she could get a good hold on the vine Sydney pulled it away from the tree as high as she could reach. Her father then grabbed onto the swinging vine and let his weight hang free, pulling the vine until it snapped. They coiled the vines and hurried back to Jordan.

"Jordan, can you hear me?" Sydney lay next to the hole with her head hanging over the edge and Dogma pressed against her side. She breathed through her mouth to lessen the smell of the rotting deer but it was still overpowering.

"We're back. My father is building a travois so we can

carry you out of here. We collected spruce boughs and creeper vines to tie the branches to the travois frame. Dad's looking for two suitable saplings for the frame now."

Sydney knew she was prattling, but she remembered being in Medicine Woman's tepee, how the sound of voices had helped pull her from the dark place she had fallen into. She wanted Jordan to know that he wasn't alone, that someone who cared was here to help him.

"Jordan? You can't die on me now. I love you, you know. I was hoping maybe you'd like to marry me. Or if we can't find anyone to legally marry us then maybe we can live together like you wanted us to do in Driftwood. Remember Driftwood, Jordan? We made some friends there. It's a nice little town. We could go back there if you wanted."

"Is your friend awake?" Sydney's father crossed the clearing with a pair of poplar saplings and set them next to the boughs and vines. He went to work assembling the simple but ingenious carrier that had been used for centuries to haul men's possessions.

"No, and I can't tell if he hears me or not. He better not die just when we get here to help him." She turned her head back toward the hole.

"You hear that, Jordan James?" she said. "You'd better not die before we get you out of there or I'm going to be furious with you."

"You love me?" Jordan's voice was barely audible, a mere shadow of his normal smooth, deep speaking voice.

A small sob of relief escaped Sydney's lips.

"Yes, you big galoot. I love you. Why'd you take off anyway? I had several squirrels for our dinner."

"Didn't. Never leave you." Jordan slipped away again.

Daniel popped into the clearing with a small hatchet in one hand and a coil of rope over one shoulder.

"This was all I could find," he said. "There's no one at the cabin." He looked at Alex's almost completed travois with admiration.

"Nice job. We'll take turns hauling him. But first we have to figure out how to get him out of that hole."

Daniel walked over to Sydney and looked down at Jordan.

"Is your friend awake?"

"His name is Jordan James," Sydney answered. "He spoke a few words, then passed out again. I need to get down there to check him over. Can you lower me on the rope?"

Daniel took the rope from his shoulder and tied one end around Sydney's chest, under her arms and over her breasts. He tugged on it.

"How does that feel?" he asked.

"It'll be all right. Dad used to take me and my twin sister rock climbing. This isn't as comfortable as a climbing harness but I don't have far to go." She was anxious to get to Jordan and see how badly he was hurt.

Daniel looped the rope around a nearby tree and walked the free end back toward Sydney.

"Ready when you are. Be careful Sydney."

Sydney took a deep breath and lowered her legs over the edge of the hole away from Jordan. She didn't want to land on top of him and worsen his injuries.

"Okay, give me some line."

Daniel played out a couple feet of rope and she slipped over the edge and dangled. She braced her hands and feet against the dirt walls of the hole.

"I'm good," she called. "Keep playing out line."

Seconds later Sydney landed on the slippery edge of the deer carcass. A burst of fresh stench overwhelmed the small space. Bile filled her throat and she bent over and vomited.

"Ugh. This is so nasty." She untied the line, let it dangle loose, and took three steps around the deer to Jordan.

Relief at finally being close enough to touch him mingled with fear as she looked at his gray face. She knelt beside him and placed her hand on his shoulder.

"Jordan," she said softly. "I'm here. Can you tell me what hurts?" She noted the blood clotted in his hair and gently ran her fingers over the back of his skull. Jordan flinched and she jerked her hand away.

"Sorry. You must have hit your head when you fell. You really should stop doing that. I'm going to feel you to see if there are any broken bones, okay? I promise I'll be careful." She didn't wait for his answer. She started at his collarbone and worked her way over his body, gently prodding for breaks.

Jordan still lay on his right side with his left arm tucked against his abdomen. She reached in and felt for his hand. He moaned when she touched his swollen wrist.

"Mmmm, either a break or a bad sprain. I hope it's just a sprain, I can fix that. Jordan can you sit up?"

No answer, then she heard a faint, "No."

Sydney took a deep breath to steady herself. She felt out of her element here, frustrated by her medical ignorance. What if Jordan died because she didn't know the right thing to do? She remembered Medicine Woman's advice to trust herself and felt a tiny bit better. The first thing they needed to do was to get Jordan back to the surface.

"Dad?" She stood and called to her father. A moment later his face appeared over the rim of the hole. A hint of a smile twitched Sydney's lips. Apparently the man who wanted to be called Alex had accepted his role as her father.

"How can we get Jordan out of here? We always had harnesses when you took me and Shannon climbing, and we were healthy and fit. Jordan isn't in any condition to give us any help."

Her father frowned then smiled. "Give me a couple more minutes. Daniel and I will lower the travois into the hole. You can lash Jordan to it and we'll haul him up." He disappeared and reappeared a minute later. The travois was carefully lowered into the hole.

Sydney guided it away from Jordan's body. "Got it," she said. She turned back to Jordan and knelt beside him.

"Jordan, I need you to stand up. Can you do that for me?"

Silence.

Sydney sighed. This would be easier if Jordan could help them. She tried to straighten his left leg but the muscles had frozen in place and resisted her efforts. She stood and looked down at him. The travois wasn't going to work. There was no way she could get Jordan upright to lash him to the carrier.

"Pull up the travois and give me more line," she called to the two men watching her. "You're going to have to pull him up with the rope." The travois disappeared. Sydney took her knife and cut the straps holding Jordan's pack to his back. She pulled it away and started to set it aside, then hesitated. She pulled the pack toward her and rummaged through it. When she found the torn strips of sheeting she gave a pleased "Yes!"

"Dad, get me my sleeping bag, please." Her father dangled the sleeping bag toward Sydney and she grabbed it, being careful to not let it touch the dead deer. She wrapped the bag lengthwise around Jordan's chest and worked the rope underneath him and then around him. She tied the bag in place and checked her knots. The bag would only provide a small amount of protection against the rope's friction, but it would help.

She then took a sheet strip and lashed Jordan's injured arm tight against his abdomen. She looked up at Daniel and her father.

"Go slow until he's fully upright, then pull him up as quickly as you can. I'll holler if you need to stop." The men's faces disappeared and the rope began to tighten until it was taut.

As Jordan slowly rose Sydney placed her arms around his torso to soften the rope's pull on his body. He reached a seated position and his head flopped forward. Sydney placed a quick kiss on his stubbly gray cheek.

"You're on your way to the surface, Jordan. We'll try not to hurt you too badly."

Jordan continued to lift and straighten until he dangled on his toes. "Okay, pull him up!" She winced as Jordan's head and front dragged against the dirt and rock on his way out of the hole. He moaned and weakly kicked one leg.

"Keep still, Jordan, you're almost free."

Jordan reached the top and stopped. Without the ability to lift his arms over the rim of the hole, his shoulders hung up on the edge. Sydney watched him lower half a foot and get pulled up, only to hang up again. The situation would be comical if it wasn't so serious.

This isn't going to work. Sydney watched Jordan with her heart in her mouth and prayed that he wasn't being hurt worse than he already was.

"Dad, wait!" she called. "You're hurting him."

Her father's face appeared at the rim. He laid on his stomach and grabbed hold of the section of rope that curled around Jordan's chest with both hands.

"Now, Daniel." Her father grunted and pulled up on Jordan's body as Daniel pulled on the rope. Jordan's torso flopped over the top edge of the hole. His legs dangled for another moment, then quickly disappeared and the rope end was tossed back down to Sydney.

She tied herself in and soon joined everyone on the surface.

"I need some warm water," she said as soon as she freed herself from the rope. She hurried to where Jordan lay, well away from the edge of hole. Dogma was licking his face, one huge paw holding him down in case he should protest.

"That's right, Dogma, he needs a cleaning." Sydney grabbed her pack and looked through the packets of medicine. Finding the two she needed, she gently untied Jordan's arm and pushed up his sleeve. The wrist was swollen and bruised but she couldn't feel any break in the bones.

"We have to move." Sydney's father spoke close behind her.

She looked up at him and realized the fine, sporadic flakes of snow had grown thicker and fatter. They covered her father's head and shoulders. The ground they had trampled and disturbed while reaching Jordan was covered with a fresh film of white.

She looked at Jordan's gray face. A thin sheen of sweat covered his forehead and nose. They needed to get Jordan to a shelter before she attempted to doctor him. She nodded at her father and stood.

"Okay. I'll tend him at the woodcutter's cabin." She replaced the packets and pulled on her pack, then grabbed Jordan's.

Jordan was strapped onto the travois and they set off down the mountain with Daniel in the lead. Behind him, Sydney's father pulled the travois with Dogma staying close by Jordan's side, and Sydney brought up the rear. Twenty minutes later they reached another small clearing. A small log cabin stood in the center.

They moved Jordan to the single cot and built a fire in the fireplace. While Sydney tended Jordan's wounds Alex stacked a pile of firewood near the door and hauled extra water from a nearby stream.

"Daniel and I have to leave you here for a while. We need to find the other two mines before the snow gets too deep." Her father gave Sydney a worried frown.

Sydney knew her father felt torn. He didn't want to leave her but he still had to fulfill his promise to help Daniel free the miners. She hugged him and smiled up into his familiar face. It didn't matter that he couldn't remember her, he was still her father and she loved him.

"We'll be fine. Go and get those poor men and boys out of the mines. They need you more than I do right now. Dogma will protect us and I'm sure I can snare a rabbit or two to feed us. Where will you take the miners? There isn't room enough here."

Daniel had been standing by the door waiting for Alex. He frowned at Sydney's question.

"You're right, we can't just leave them in the woods. We'll have to take them to the temple. They'll have food and plenty of room for the miners. Besides, from what some of the boys said, a few of them have mothers at the temple."

Alex hugged Sydney back and looked down into her face. "I'll help the miners get to the temple and then come back here for you and Jordan. Don't try to move him before I return."

Sydney smiled. "Yes, Daddy. Whatever you say," she replied in a mocking tone. Then more seriously, "I promise we'll wait here for you. Don't worry about us, we're used to surviving odd situations."

Her father ruffled her hair.

"That's my girl. Come on, Daniel, let's get those poor souls out of those mines."

Within moments Sydney was left alone with Jordan and Dogma. The great beast lay in front of the warm fire, stretched out, and was soon snoring lightly. Sydney bent down and scratched her belly.

"You did good, Dogma," she whispered. "You helped us find him. You saved his life."

Sydney set a stool next to the cot. She hoped Daniel and her father would be able to free the miners without bloodshed and said a little prayer for the prisoners' health.

She took Jordan's uninjured hand in her own and settled in to wait.

17

THREE DAYS PASSED. Sydney treated Jordan's sprain with wormwood and goldenrod and his head wound with a decoction made from the wood and inner bark of white pine, a mixture Medicine Woman claimed would clean any infected flesh.

She forced some of the healing broth into him during the short periods Jordan was awake. She made brief forays outside for firewood and food, and to look for her father and Daniel. It worried her that they hadn't returned yet, but she had no idea what condition they had found the miners in. It might have taken them days to get the younger boys to the temple.

By day three Jordan was sitting up, but instead of the cheerful companion she remembered, he acted sullen and ill-tempered. When he refused to eat any of the rabbit she had caught and roasted over the fire for him, Sydney threw up her hands in disgust.

"What the devil is wrong with you?" she demanded, setting a portion of the rabbit in front of Dogma, who was only too happy to wolf down the treat.

"I've never known you to be so cranky. I'm beginning to wonder if we should've left you in that hole."

"Yeah, you shoulda," muttered Jordan.

"What!?" Sydney fisted her hands on her hips and glared at him. "What do you mean, 'we shoulda' left you? Are you insane? Did your brains leak out that new bump on your head?"

Jordan jutted his chin out and a stubborn look came over his face.

"I'm not insane. I've finally come to my senses. Lying down in that hole I realized what a burden I've been to you. Having to look after yourself in this crazy world is tough enough; having to look after a blind man as well is too much to ask of anyone. I was wrong to trap you in my storm cellar and wrong to force my company on you. I can take care of myself from now on."

Sydney's mouth opened and closed. She couldn't believe they were having this conversation. She thought Jordan loved her. She narrowed her eyes at him. It was too bad he couldn't see how pissed off he was making her. Maybe if he knew how mad she felt he'd smarten up and stop spouting nonsense.

"So what are you saying, Jordan?" Her voice became dangerously soft. "After all we've been through together you think that it's time we parted ways?" She lowered her face close to Jordan's ear. She wanted to be sure he heard every word she had to say.

"Now you listen to me, piano man. You're not going anywhere without me. You understand? I love you. I just found my father, and I have a whole new family that now includes you, Dogma, and Grandmother and Daniel."

Jordan tried to speak and she laid a finger across his lips.

"Let me make myself perfectly clear, Jordan James. I don't

want any misunderstanding between us. You aren't going anywhere without me. Period. End of discussion. Do you understand?"

Jordan reached up with his good hand and pulled Sydney's finger from his lips. He kissed the palm of her hand and then pulled her down onto his lap.

"You love me?" He wrapped his uninjured arm around her and pulled her tight against him.

"You really, honest-to-Betsy love me?" he asked again. The feeling of inadequacy that had been plaguing him since he woke in the cabin vanished.

"Yes, you idiot, I love you. I have never felt so empty and hurt as I did when I thought you'd left me," she whispered against his neck. "I thought we had something together and then you up and left without a word."

Jordan planted small, gentle kisses over Sydney's hair and her forehead.

"I didn't leave," he said. "I was kidnapped and taken to the crazy Temple of Gaia." He stopped kissing her and lifted his head.

"Wait, did you say you found your father and grand-mother? I thought they were both dead. And who is Daniel?"

It dawned on Sydney that Jordan knew nothing about finding her father, or about Daniel and Medicine Woman. They hadn't had any opportunity to talk as Jordan had been unconscious since they pulled him from the hole. No wonder he was talking crazy.

She snuggled against him, her anger forgotten, and filled him in on all that had happened to her since they parted ways. When she told Jordan how she had nearly died and that Medicine Woman had been forced to amputate two of her toes and part of a finger he groaned and pulled her tighter against him.

"I'm so sorry," he said. "I could see my kidnapper's auras but they never spoke. I didn't realize I was being taken by a group of women or I would have resisted. Thank heavens your father found you when he did. I couldn't bear it if you had died alone. I'm sorry he doesn't remember you. You must find that very frustrating."

Sydney shrugged. "My father is the same good and kind man I remember from before his head injury. He treats me well and he believes my claim that I'm his daughter. Under the circumstances I'll take whatever he offers and be happy. You'll meet him and Daniel when they return from the temple."

Jordan stiffened. He wanted nothing to do with the crazy Temple of Gaia.

"Why are they going to the temple?"

Sydney told him her father and Daniel had gone to rescue the young boys and kidnapped men who were being held in the gold mines.

"That's not good," said Jordan, and he explained about the Solstice Ceremony and the woodcutter named Big Mike who planned to steal the High Priestess's hoard of gold.

"We need to get to the temple," he said when he'd finished. "Big Mike has no scruples about eliminating anyone who gets in his way. He's been waiting for more than five years for an opportunity to snatch Mallory Dunne's gold. He won't hesitate to hurt or kill your father and Daniel if they try to stop him."

Sydney sat up straight and looked into Jordan's worried eyes.

"I'm sure Dad and Daniel can handle one man."

"They might not recognize the danger. Big Mike acted like my friend right up until the moment he pushed me down that test hole. He pretends to be a lowly woodcutter, but I think he was also one of the men who guarded the miners. And they don't call him Big Mike for nothing. The man is huge. His aura loomed over me and I'm over six foot."

Sydney stood and crossed the cabin to her backpack. "I'll go warn them," she said while she rolled up her sleeping bag and secured it to her pack.

"You stay here. You can't travel yet. I'll leave wood by the door and the rest of the rabbit stew. It will hold you until I return. The temple can't be very far from here. I should be able to get there and back by morning."

"Sydney."

Sydney stopped packing and looked up. Jordan was on his feet and scowling at her.

"Didn't we just agree that we would stick together?" he asked.

"Well, yes, but this is different. You shouldn't travel and I need to warn my father."

Jordan crossed the room and pulled Sydney to her feet.

She barely registered the fact that he had zeroed in on her as accurately as any sighted man.

"I'm coming with you or you're not going. Those are your only two choices. Which will it be?"

Sydney looked up into Jordan's determined face. His steely gray eyes looked down at her and she knew he meant every word. They would go together or not at all. She stood on tiptoe and kissed him lightly on the moth.

"Okay, you win. We go together. I'll get everything packed and put out the fire."

It took very little time to pack up their meager belongings. Sydney rigged new strips on Jordan's pack to replace the ones she'd cut, then handed him his staff and ushered him outside, where they strapped on the makeshift snowshoes she had fashioned for their trip back to Medicine Woman's camp.

The snowstorm that had begun three days ago while they were rescuing Jordan had lasted a day and a night, dumping over twenty inches of fresh, fluffy snow on the mountains.

Sydney's homemade snowshoes were nothing like the high-tech aluminum pair she had left behind at her grandfather's farm, but they worked. Made from thin saplings bent into a frame with the ends lashed together, she had cut strips from one of the deer hides she found in the cabin and wove the strips to the frame until she had created an open platform.

Her first attempt was a failure as she forgot to leave a toe hole, forcing her to lift each shoe, an action that would quickly tire out the wearer. She took the faulty shoes apart and remade them with a hole for her toe, a design that allowed her heel to lift off the shoe so she could slide them forward instead of lifting them. The shoes were crude, but effective.

Jordan had no difficulty learning how to walk in the snowshoes, reminding Sydney that he had been an athlete before he lost his sight. She led the way, following a trail through the woods that seemed the most heavily traveled from the cabin's clearing. Their progress was slowed by the fact that Sydney had to break trail in the snow for Jordan and Dogma to follow.

They both fell more than once while Dogma bounded gleefully through the snow like a wave of gray canine fur. Naked branches stood tall and still against the deep blue sky. Snow crystals glittered under the sun's rays and turned the mountainside into a shimmering jewel. Sydney found the journey a pleasant adventure except for the possible danger that awaited them at their destination.

After several hours she heard the sound of falling water.

"I hear the falls," said Jordan. "The temple is a half mile beyond them. If we stick to the trail once we cross the stream they'll see us coming. I think we should stay on this side until nightfall and then try to sneak in and see what's going on."

Sydney hesitated. Crossing a stream in the dark could be dangerous. If one of them fell in, even Dogma, they could freeze to death.

As if sensing her thoughts, Jordan reassured her.

"There's a crude bridge—Dogma and I crossed it when we made our escape. We can check to see if it's still there and you can try it in daylight first. Or if you see a place for us to keep out of sight on the other side we can cross it now."

They moved forward carefully. Sydney watched the woods for any sign of movement. Jordan also checked for human auras moving amongst the trees but no one was about. They crossed the unsteady bridge without incident and settled into a stand of spruce trees to wait for nightfall.

While they waited Jordan told Sydney everything he could remember about the temple and the people in it. She felt amazed and humbled by the details he picked up during his stay. The pictures he painted with his senses gave her a clear image of the place. The only thing missing was color.

"Jordan," she said suddenly, "do you dream in color or black and white and gray?"

Jordan thought for a moment.

"I never really thought about it. But I think I used to dream in black and white, and recently I started dreaming in color. I had a dream about you while I was trapped. In my dream I could see your green eyes and black hair and your dusky skin. That's the first technicolor dream I can remember having."

"That's amazing. You described me perfectly. How could

you know?"

Jordan chuckled. "Not so amazing, I'm afraid. You described yourself to me that morning at Doc Melody's, remember? I never forgot. Between your words and my touch I built up an image of you that I've carried with me ever since. I just never really saw it until that dream."

They sat in companionable silence and watched the light change the snow from white to pale blue as the sun dipped lower in the sky.

"There's something else different now, too," said Jordan. "While I was in the hole I opened my eyes once and saw the walls glowing a dull purple. I didn't think anything of it because I'd hit my head pretty hard and I figured I had a concussion and was hallucinating. The crazy thing is, today I've been able to see not only your and Dogma's auras, and the auras of the trees and plants, but I can see the auras of rocks and dirt. It's like I can see the whole world again, just not the way other people can. I've turned into some sort of aura-reading freak."

Sydney slipped off her mitten and cupped Jordan's cheek with her hand.

"Nah, you're not a freak. You've simply gained some skills that the rest of the world doesn't have. You've become more than any of us could ever be. That makes you very, very special." She kissed him lightly on the lips. "At least you're very special to me, Jordan," she whispered.

Jordan kissed her back and Sydney wished they weren't standing outside in the snow. She'd like to follow their kisses to whatever came next. She broke of the kiss with a reluctant sigh and replaced her mitten.

"You'll have to lead us into the temple. You see better in the dark than I do and you know where we're going. The sun is setting, it's time to move."

18

THE DISTANCE from the falls to the temple was shorter than Jordan remembered. Maybe that's because he really didn't want to go back there. They proceeded with caution until they were assured that no one was outside, then walked quietly up the steps and onto the porch.

"This place is beautiful," whispered Sydney. "It's a gigantic lodge built of logs. Whoever built this place must have spent a fortune on it."

They removed their snowshoes and backpacks and leaned them against the wall, then tiptoed to the massive front door and listened. Behind them, the full moon rose from the land and lit up the snow-covered landscape. No other light was needed to see by. The moonlight reflecting off the snow shone brighter than a cloudy day.

"I don't see any lit windows," said Sydney, her voice low. She felt nervous and a little afraid. What if the temple acolytes captured her and Jordan? The moon was full and today was the winter solstice. And here was Jordan, back at the temple he had bravely escaped from.

"Jordan, wait." She pulled him away from the door so they wouldn't be heard if someone passed by the other side.

"*Why* did the acolytes kidnap you? What were they going to do with you and why was today so important?"

"They, uh, they…well, it's a little hard to explain," answered Jordan. He didn't want to tell Sydney about the ceremony and his part in establishing the next group of miners.

"Jordan. Tell me. Just spit it out."

"Crap. All right, I'll tell you. Mallory Dunne, the High Priestess, needed a sperm donor for her girls. She kidnapped me for this year's Father of the Year."

Sydney's mouth dropped open.

"You can't be serious. That's *insane*," she hissed.

"I know. I agree. Ruby, one of the acolytes, told me that Mallory brings in a man every year to, uh, impregnate some of the women. Can we drop the subject and try to find your father now?"

Sydney's eyes narrowed. Jordan was *her* man. Mallory Dunne, High Priestess or no, had no right to kidnap him for her wicked scheme. Just wait until she got her hands on the crazy woman.

"Yes, we can drop it," she said aloud. "I can't wait to meet this Miss Dunne. I'm definitely going to have words with your High Priestess." She sprinted back toward the temple's front door.

Jordan caught up with Sydney and grabbed her arm.

"Wait a sec, you can't just go barging in there. Mallory is dangerous. There's gold involved, remember? She'll protect her gold from any threat, even if it means killing innocent people. And don't forget, this is a cult. The acolytes will do whatever she tells them. She has them brainwashed; they believe whatever she says is the truth."

Sydney fumed for a moment, then took her hand off the doorknob.

"You're right. I let my temper get the better of me. What's our plan?"

Jordan thought for a minute.

"The ceremony will take place in the large meeting room —I think. With the sun down and the moon up, I'd hazard a guess that it's already started. That means everyone will be together. We'll search the rest of the temple until we find the miners and your father, then tell your father about Big Mike and the gold."

"Okay. I trust you. Lead on."

Jordan could hear the evil grin in Sydney's voice. It warmed him to know that she felt outraged at the way Mallory had intended to use him. She sounded a little jealous as well and he found that he liked that. If Sydney felt jealousy then she truly meant it when she claimed she loved him. The knowledge warmed him. He slowly opened the front door and slid inside the temple.

Sydney followed Jordan through the door and looked around the massive foyer in awe. The floor was tiled in an intricate pattern of deep green and tan, the walls stuccoed in a warm brick red. The ceiling rose above her too many stories to count and was lost in the darkness overhead.

"Holy cow," she whispered.

Jordan put his finger to his lips and pointed down the hallway to the right. "

The meeting room is down there." He turned to his left.

"Let's start this way. You lead."

Sydney headed toward the wide hallway with Dogma close on her heels. As soon as they left the foyer the floor turned to carpet which muffled the sound of their steps, allowing them to move faster. Sydney opened each door on the left side of the hall. All the rooms showed signs that women lived in them, but they were empty.

The trio reached the end of the hall and headed back toward the foyer, this time checking each room on the opposite side with the same results. They checked the room next to the foyer and then listened for anyone moving about. Sydney heard the faint sound of women's voices raised in chanting or singing; she couldn't quite tell which.

"There's a central hall opposite the front door," whispered Jordan. "I saw people come and go through it whenever Lorelei took me outside. Do you see it? Let's try down that way."

Sydney led the way across the foyer and entered another carpeted hall. This time Sydney crossed back and forth, checking each room before moving further away from the foyer. Just like in the first hall, all the rooms were being used but empty.

She frowned when they reached the far end.

"Jordan, where did they keep you when you were here?"

Jordan pointed up.

"Upstairs. During the warm months the cult uses the whole lodge, but once it gets cold they all move down to the rooms on the main floor. Knowing Mallory's dislike for men, that's probably where they would house the miners. She wouldn't waste heat on them."

Sydney found an emergency stairwell that led to the upper floors. Jordan followed her up the stairs with Dogma bringing up the rear, her toenails clicking on the concrete stairs. Sydney could hear Dogma panting and hoped that it wasn't loud enough to draw someone's attention.

They checked every room on both upper floors but found no sign of the miners, nor of Daniel and Sydney's father. When they opened the door to Jordan's old room he recognized it immediately. The window he had broken hadn't been repaired, and a cold breeze blew through the broken pane and into the hall.

"This was my room," said Jordan. He shivered and refused to go in.

Sydney stepped inside and looked around. She noted the overturned chair with a spring stretched out, the naked mattress and shards of broken glass on the floor. Anger washed over her. How arrogant and cruel of the High Priestess to hold a blind man hostage for her crazy scheme. Sydney hoped she would get a chance to tell Mallory Dunne just what she thought of her.

She spotted a long, jagged shard of glass partially hidden under the bed and stooped to pick it up. Several strips of sheeting lay nearby. She grabbed one and wrapped it around the fat end of the glass shard, fashioning a crude weapon. It might slow someone down if they were caught and attacked by the cult.

Sydney took one last look at the room that had been Jordan's prison and rejoined her companions in the hall.

"Now what?" she asked. "It doesn't look as if Daniel and Dad have made it here with the miners yet. Either they've been delayed or Mallory is holding them somewhere else. Is there a barn?"

Jordan leaned against the wall and slid to a seated position. His head and wrist were throbbing. Dogma sat, pressed up against his side and pushed her wet nose into his neck. He scratched and tugged gently on her ear while he considered what he knew of the lodge and the cult.

"We haven't checked the rooms near Mallory's suite. If we go back to the foyer we'll have to pass the meeting room and someone will see us. Maybe there's another emergency stairwell that will take us down the back way." He struggled to stand and moaned when he tried to put weight on his wrist.

Sydney reached down and took his good hand and braced herself.

"Pull against me, Jordan, don't use your injured arm if you can help it."

On the third attempt Jordan gained his feet. He held his injured wrist against his body.

"Wait here." Sydney went back into Jordan's old room and grabbed the other sheet strip from the floor. She made a crude sling for his wrist and secured it against his chest.

"That should help. You can't use it anyway and this way you won't accidentally knock it against something."

They went in search of a back stair and found what they needed at the end of the hallway that teed off the central hall. When they reached the first floor Sydney cracked open the door a few narrow inches, enough to see if anyone stood guard outside the meeting room.

The sound of chanting—she could distinguish it now—sounded louder here, but the hall appeared to be empty. Apparently Mallory felt confident that no one would crash her solstice celebration.

Sydney eased the stairwell door open further and squeezed through it. She held the door for Jordan and Dogma to follow, then pulled it quietly closed behind them. They made their way toward the meeting room, stopping at each room to look for the men.

At the fourth room door Sydney stopped and pressed her ear against it.

"I hear someone in here," she whispered. "This must be where they put the miners."

Before Jordan could speak she opened the door and stepped inside. Her mouth dropped open in amazement at the sight of the huge man standing at the window opposite. A quick survey of the rest of the room told her no one else was there.

Jordan and Dogma pushed into the room behind her.

"Sydney, I recognize Mallory's scent. I think this is her suite. She wouldn't keep the miners—ah crap," Jordan said. "I thought you'd be out of here by now, Big Mike." He moved to stand beside Sydney. Next to him, Dogma growled low in her throat.

"Jordan! What a surprise. Not a pleasant one I'm afraid. Sometime when I'm not in so much of a hurry you'll have to tell me how you escaped the test shaft. I know that hole was too deep for you to climb out of."

Big Mike crossed the room swiftly and locked the door behind them.

"Should've done that when I came in. Careless of me." He grabbed a folded blanket from the couch and tossed it over Dogma's head, then pushed her into the bathroom and shut the door. The great beast began to whine and bark.

"Damn dog. Fortunately I'm almost finished here. You're right, Jordan, I should be long gone, but Mallory had other ideas since her Stud of the Year went missing." He crossed the room to the side chamber and reappeared a moment later with a heavy brown cloth sack. Returning to the window, he tossed the sack outside.

"That does it. I'd love to stick around and visit but this is the first opportunity I've had to get to the gold. They'll come looking for me soon. I still have one more part to play in their little ceremony. Too bad I won't be here, but you will, Jordan. Maybe you'll get to be Father of the Year after all."

Sydney looked at the side chamber door and saw that the frame had been splintered near the lock. That was where Mallory kept her gold, she realized. She let out a sigh of relief. If Big Mike was finished and leaving then they could get out of here as well. There was no point in sticking around since the miners weren't here yet.

Big Mike veered across the room until he stood in front of Jordan and Sydney. He lashed out quickly and landed a quick jab to Sydney's face. As she crumbled to the floor he picked her up, tossed her over his shoulder and crossed back to the window.

"My insurance," Big Mike called over his shoulder to Jordan as he stuck one leg out the window.

"I'll let her go once I'm sure no one is following me." Then he was gone.

Jordan stood in unbelieving shock for several moments. Had Big Mike just hit Sydney? An angry flush unstuck his feet and he carefully made his way across the room to the still open window. Jordan leaned his uninjured hand on the sill and stuck his head out into the cold night.

Big Mike's aura was already moving off to the left, away from the lodge and toward the woods. A smaller aura lay behind the big man. Jordan frowned in puzzlement, then realized Mike must be using a sled to transport the gold. Sydney lay on the sled. Jordan couldn't tell if she was lying down because Mike threatened her, or if Mike had knocked her unconscious.

Big Mike had already covered half the distance to the woods. Jordan worked one leg out the open window and felt only empty air. He stretched his toe down as far as he could reach but still felt nothing. How far down was the ground? He couldn't risk breaking a leg—then he would be unable to chase after Sydney. It would be smarter to leave the lodge by the front door, grab his snowshoes, and follow the kidnapper.

Jordan knew that he could sneak up on the big man at

night, when his special vision would help him see what the other man could not. But he had to get moving before he lost sight of them.

Behind him Dogma yowled. Jordan had forgotten all about the great beast.

"Dogma, quiet!" He'd better let her out of the bathroom before she brought the entire cult running. He closed the window and followed the wall until he found the bathroom door and released the frustrated canine.

She gave a sharp bark and sniffed the room, headed straight to the window, and then barked again.

"That scumbag took Sydney hostage, Dogma. We're going to have to leave by the front door." Dogma joined him by the bathroom and pressed against his leg. Jordan took a moment to orient himself in the room and grabbed her ruff, but before he could cross the room the door opened. Jordan froze.

"Well, Master James. I never expected to see you and your beastly dog again. What are you doing in my room?" The door slammed shut behind Mallory.

Mallory's cloying scent filled the room. Jordan fought the urge to gag. He needed Mallory to let him leave; it wouldn't do to piss her off.

"Big Mike just robbed you and took my girlfriend hostage. Get out of my way, I have to go after them." He took a step toward her. Mallory's aura flared with unmistakable anger and Jordan heard the door lock click.

"You're not going anywhere, Master James. You're the only one who knew where I stored the gold. Nobody robs me or betrays my trust and gets away with it."

"You don't understand." The overwhelming urge to strangle the crazy woman before him made Jordan's hands itch.

"I saw Big Mike when I escaped. I thought he was a good man and I told him about your gold. He just robbed you, Mallory. He took my friend hostage. I have to go after him."

"Sit down, Master James. *I said* you aren't going anywhere."

19

Jordan clenched his jaw and considered his options. He could overpower the High Bitch, or even sic Dogma on her. But he'd never been a violent man and both those ideas made him feel ill. He decided to appeal to Mallory Dunne's greed.

"I'll return the gold that Big Mike stole from you. I promise. But I need to leave now, before they get too far away."

"I told you to sit down, Master James. I have a ceremony to conduct. I'll deal with you when I've finished. I'll be placing guards, one at the door and one outside under the window, so don't even think about trying to leave before I return." Her nails dug into the flesh of Jordan's arm as she led him to a chair.

He refused to sit.

"I'm not waiting here for you," he said defiantly. "My friend needs me and I'm going after her, even if it means hurting one of your guards."

Mallory leaned closer to Jordan. Her robes felt cool and silky as they brushed against his hand. He retreated a step and came up against the chair. She pushed on his chest. Caught off balance, Jordan abruptly sat.

"I'll be back after the ceremony," Mallory said, just as if she'd never heard him. "We have some unfinished business I believe."

"What about your gold?" asked Jordan. Why wasn't Mallory more angry? Her whole world was built around the gold mines and the attainment of wealth and power. How could she act so blasé about the robbery?

"Never fear, I will get my gold back, Master James," said Mallory. "And you will be punished for betraying me."

A loud commotion broke out in the hall. Mallory crossed to the hall door and flung it open.

"What's going on out here? Why aren't you all waiting in the meeting room as I requested? How did *you* get in here?"

Jordan could hear feminine voices raised in the hall. Excited voices mixed with a few that sounded angry. Then he heard male voices speaking over the women. Daniel and Sydney's father had finally arrived with the miners.

"Time for us to leave, Dogma." Jordan pushed past Mallory and into the hall. A hand grabbed his jacket. He jerked free and squeezed through the throng with Dogma pressed tight against his side. The rank odor of sweat and dirt mixed in with the clean, soapy scent of the women assaulted his nose.

Which one of these men was Sydney's father? he wondered.

"I'm looking for Alex Waters," he said loudly. "Alex Waters, are you here?"

A woman knelt in front of him holding onto a short aura and crying. A mother reunited with her son, Jordan realized, and felt a momentary satisfaction that Daniel and Sydney's father had succeeded at their task. Now that the cult members knew that Mallory sent their children to die in the mines perhaps they would no longer follow her.

He worked his way around the crying mother and called Alex's name again.

"I'm Alex Waters, Jordan. Give me your arm and I'll guide you out of this mess to a quieter spot. What are you doing here? Where's Sydney? I thought she'd be with you. It's not like my daughter to abandon her patient."

Jordan waited until they cleared the noisy crowd before he answered Alex. Another male aura joined them.

"Jordan, this is our friend Daniel. His great grandmother saved Sydney's life. Where *is* my daughter?" Both men sounded bone weary. They told Jordan that the snowstorm had made travel difficult with the weakened miners, especially the younger boys, and they had been forced to carry several of them in a series of relays from the mines to the lodge.

Jordan quickly told them about Big Mike stealing Mallory's gold and taking Sydney hostage.

"We need to go after him before he gets too far away," he said, starting down the hall.

Sydney's father placed a hand on Jordan's shoulder.

"Daniel and I will find her, son. We'll be able to move faster if we don't have to worry about you. No offense, but I imagine you're still recovering from your ordeal."

Jordan gritted his teeth. He knew that Alex was only trying to be kind. He also knew that what Sydney's father really meant was that he and Daniel could travel faster without a blind man tagging along. He would have to tell them about his second sight if he wanted them to treat him as they would a sighted man.

"I can see in the dark better than either of you can," Jordan said quietly. He didn't want his secret to be overheard.

"I see the energy fields of living things. It doesn't matter if it's day or night. I can follow Big Mike in the dark, through forest or cave, because I can see his aura. He won't escape me."

Daniel spoke first. "I've heard that certain people can see the auras of others. Can you also see the auras of animals and plants?"

"Yes. And more recently, after the last bump on the head, I see the aura of dirt and rocks. The whole planet is one gigantic living being." They were wasting time discussing this. Jordan was ready to go *now*, but he knew the two men needed to accept him as an equal, not a man they saw as handicapped.

"My grandfather Smokey sees auras," said Daniel. "You have been truly blessed, Jordan. Alex, I think we would be wise to bring him with us."

"All right then, let's get going," said Alex. "What direction did they head off in, Jordan?"

Jordan didn't answer right away. The mysterious Smokey was Daniel's *grandfather.* An old man. The same man Sydney had been trying to find for months now. *He was an old man.* Jordan smiled as his fear that Sydney would leave him once she found her friend Smokey trickled away like sand through his fingers. Now only Big Mike stood between Jordan and the woman he loved.

Sydney's eyes fluttered open as her body was jolted sideways, then righted itself. Winter-naked branches passed overhead, reaching towards a starry sky. She tried to raise her hand to feel her aching jaw but she couldn't lift her arms. She struggled to sit without any success. Big Mike had lashed her to his sled.

She moaned as the sled hit another rough spot and hard, lumpy shapes dug into her back and thighs. The stolen gold. She was lying on top of the stolen gold. Big Mike had punched her and taken her hostage.

She wondered how long she had been unconscious. How far were they from the lodge? She turned her head from side to side until she spotted the moon dropping behind the mountaintop. At least two hours had passed, judging by the moon's position.

Her fingers and toes were numb with cold. She needed to get moving before frostbite claimed any more of them. She struggled against the ropes again but they held tight. The sled shushed through the snow in fits and starts, matching Big Mike's steps.

"I won't be much of a hostage if I die on you," she called to her abductor. She heard a deep chuckle.

"So, the little lady awakens. How's your chin? I hit you pretty hard, but I needed to knock you out and I didn't have time for finesse."

He didn't sound at all sorry, nor did he apologize for punching Sydney in the face. What a jerk. She felt anger, but it was directed more at herself than at Big Mike. How could she have let him take her hostage? She'd been careless, taken by surprise. She hoped Jordan and Dogma were okay.

"I'm going to get frostbite if I don't get my arms and legs moving. How about untying me? I'll walk alongside the sled, I promise." She received a short bark of laughter in response to her request.

"Nah, I don't think that's a good idea," said Big Mike. "I don't have time to chase you down if you run away. Now keep quiet or I'll be forced to gag you."

Sydney bit back her retort. Big Mike obviously didn't care about her welfare. I'm a hostage, she reminded herself.

Hostages are expendable. It doesn't matter what condition I'm in. When the end comes he's going to either kill me and or abandon me somewhere where he knows I'll die.

A single tear leaked out of the side of her eye ands ran toward her ear. She wasn't ready to die. She had her father and Jordan and she was learning to be a healer. She thought about the two men left in her life. Jordan wouldn't give up on her, and when her father returned from the mine he would come looking for her as well. She needed to stay alive until they found her.

***

The three men and Dogma hadn't quite reached the lodge's front door when Jordan heard his name called. He tried to ignore it but she called again, louder this time.

"Jordan, wait!"

"Lorelei?" Jordan turned briefly when he recognized her voice.

"We can't stop. Big Mike has Sydney and he has a head start on us." He turned away from Lorelei and stepped toward the door. They didn't have time for interruptions, every lost moment took Sydney farther away from him.

"Jordan, hold up a minute." Lorelei caught his sleeve and pulled until Jordan stopped.

"I want to thank your friends for freeing the men from the mines. We had no idea what Mallory was up to." A sob caught her and she steadied her voice.

"I owe you an apology as well. It was wrong to hold you captive here. I'm sorry I played a part in it."

"You're forgiven. Now will you let us go, please? Big Mike's taken Sydney hostage and we need to go after him."

"Big Mike? The woodcutter, you mean. I don't know who

Sydney is but you'll need snowshoes to chase after him. Wait here, I'll be back in a minute."

Jordan didn't want to wait but Lorelei's aura disappeared before he could tell her they were leaving. He felt a man's hand on his arm.

"Relax, Jordan," Sydney's father said. "We'll find her. Give the young lady a minute or two. I have a feeling she's about to make our task easier."

Lorelei took closer to five minutes. Jordan couldn't bear the wait. He was almost to the door when she called to him again.

"Jordan, wait! These will make it easier for you to move through the snow. The lodge is equipped with a wide assortment of winter toys, including the latest in snowshoe designs. I brought a pair for each of you. Mr. Waters, and Mr. Daniel, I can't thank you enough for what you've done." She handed out the snowshoes and gave Jordan a quick hug.

"Godspeed."

The men carried the snowshoes outside and strapped them on. In the interest of saving time Jordan swallowed his pride and allowed Daniel to help him strap his snowshoes to his boots.

Jordan figured that hauling the sled, made heavy with the weight of the gold and Sydney, would slow Big Mike's pace. He pushed Dogma forward, encouraging her to follow Sydney and Mike's scent. Daniel confirmed that they were following a sled track and they set off after the pair with Jordan and Dogma in the lead.

Jordan knew his companions were beyond exhausted after their ordeal with the miners, but he didn't dare slow his pace. He knew Big Mike now, and he held no doubts that the woodcutter would dispose of Sydney as soon as he felt safe from pursuit. They had to find him before he either killed Sydney outright or tossed her over a cliff.

They followed Big Mike's trail for several hours. The night grew bitter cold and dry. Every breath of air felt harsh in Jordan's nose and lungs. His admiration for his companion's stamina and determination grew with every step forward. Neither man uttered a complaining word. They suffered in silence and kept pace with Dogma and Jordan.

These were men he'd be proud to call friends, Jordan thought as they scrambled down a short incline. A few minutes later he spotted the woodcutter's aura traveling over a mostly clear patch below and in front of them. Sydney's smaller aura lay horizontal behind Big Mike.

"There they are!" He pointed at the pair and grinned. "We should be able to catch up in another fifteen or twenty minutes." The men quickened their pace and dropped down to Big Mike's level.

"What happens when we catch up?" asked Daniel. "Is this guy armed?"

"I don't know," admitted Jordan. "It doesn't matter. There are three of us and only one of him. Plus Dogma. He may be a giant, but we can take him."

"What if he threatens to hurt Sydney?" Alex asked. "That's the whole point of taking a hostage—to use as a bargaining chip."

"Then we bargain," said Jordan. "We don't care about the gold, we just want Sydney back. Big Mike doesn't care about Sydney, he just wants the gold. We'll let him leave with the gold as long as he leaves Sydney with us, unharmed." Jordan felt confidant Big Mike would go for that deal.

They pressed on and drew closer. The trees thinned out and nearly disappeared. Jordan could tell by the way the tree's auras dropped away below him that they were crossing a steep, naked bowl, perhaps the remnants of a rockslide created during an earthquake. A few small saplings struggled to take hold on the steep slope.

Jordan watched Big Mike's aura halt, then jerk forward, then halt again. Sydney's aura slid sideways and Jordan's heart leaped into his throat. Did the big man have enough strength to hang onto the heavy sled on this steep slant?

He hurried forward with Dogma on his heels, then stopped. This was not the place to attack Big Mike. If he lost his hold on the sled Sydney would be doomed.

Jordan slowed and waited for Daniel and Alex's father to catch up.

"We'll get him on the other side of this bowl," he said, keeping his voice low so Big Mike wouldn't hear him.

"We may have no choice," Daniel answered. "It looks like the woodcutter is getting rid of Sydney."

Jordan whirled around. It took him a moment to make sense of what he saw. Big Mike had braced the sled against a small tree and his aura leaned over Sydney. Suddenly he stood tall with Sydney's struggling form in his arms and tossed her down the steep slope.

"I'll get Sydney!" Alex squatted low on his heels and slid down the embankment after his daughter.

Jordan gave a strangled cry and shuffled forward as fast as the snowshoes would allow. His left foot caught a buried limb and he fell face down in the snow.

Dogma snaked in front of him, running low to the ground in attack mode. She reached Big Mike and launched herself at him with a snarl, then darted off. Her instincts were strong. This was the way her ancestors had fought, darting and snapping at their prey until they weakened from blood loss. Only then did they move in to kill.

Daniel reached down and pulled Jordan to his feet, then

took off after Dogma. Big Mike's curses ripped through the still air as he tried to block Dogma's slashing attacks.

Jordan ran after Daniel, consumed by an overwhelming need to destroy Big Mike, to annihilate the man who had hurt and then stolen the most precious thing in Jordan's life.

Daniel beat Jordan to the woodcutter and leaped on Big Mike's back. He tried to bring him down but Big Mike easily shook off the tired teen.

A moment later Jordan watched the wily woodcutter escape down the hill on his sled.

Big Mike let out a laughing "Yee-Haw!" and then suddenly dropped from sight with a loud scream.

"Daniel! What happened? Where'd he go?" Jordan helped Daniel to his feet.

"He must have gone over a drop-off," Daniel replied. "Crazy idiot. Anyone who spends time in the mountains knows that there are always hidden ravines and cliffs."

"Drop-off?" Panic filled Jordan's chest.

"Where's Sydney and Alex?" he asked.

2 0

Sydney's feet dangled in the air. The thin sapling she had caught and wrapped her arms around was the only thing between her and certain death. The surge of hope she had felt when Big Mike untied her from his sled had quickly turned to terror when he tossed her down the steep slope.

She buried her face against her arms and tried to think of a way out of her predicament. Only her father's training had saved her from tumbling into oblivion. He had drilled emergency routines into her head until they became instinct.

She heard Big Mike's victorious shout as he sledded by her, then a scream and crash sounded from somewhere below.

"Sydney."

She was already hallucinating from the cold. Soon her arms would grow too tired to bear her weight and she would join Big Mike.

"Sydney, look at me."

"I can't," she sobbed. "You're not really here and I can't bear it. I'm going to die alone, just as I deserve, just as Shannon did." She felt a hand grasp her right arm and caught her breath. She was experiencing a very real hallucination.

"I'm here, daughter. You're going to be all right. Trust me. Hold my hand."

"I can't. My hands are too cold and numb. I can't feel my fingers." Slowly Sydney lifted her head. Her father sat in the snow above her.

"Daddy."

"I'm here," her father said. "We're going to crawl out of this bowl at an angle. I want you to use my body and climb above me so that if you slip I'll be able to catch you. Okay?"

Sydney nodded. She pulled up her legs while her father pulled on her arms. Inch by inch she moved above the precipice, then finally above her father. He kept up a running patter of encouragement as they crawled side by side out of the bowl and finally joined Dogma, Jordan, and Daniel off to the side in the trees.

Jordan grabbed hold of Sydney and buried his cold nose in her neck. "I was terrified that I'd lost you," he murmured.

"My father trained me and Shannon to spread-eagle against the ground if we ever fell down a steep slope while climbing. He must have taught me well because I did it without even thinking and it slowed me down enough to grab onto a small tree."

"Your father is brilliant," said Daniel.

"Yes he is," Sydney agreed.

The trip back to the lodge was long but uneventful. The snow had been tramped flat by so many feet that Sydney had no problem walking without snowshoes. When they reached the lodge they found the acolytes and miners settled in the dining room. They took turns standing over the heating vents to thaw their chilled bodies, then joined the miners and ate hot soup and warm biscuits.

Blankets and pillows were fetched from the upper unheated rooms, and the miners and Sydney's group spread out on the dining room floor for the night. Despite soaking her hands in tepid water, the throbbing pain in Sydney's hands as her circulation returned prevented her from falling asleep.

She listened to the sounds of the men around her. Two snored heavily, great big nasally snorts that sounded nothing like sawing logs. Whoever had made that comparison had apparently never heard snores like these.

Across the room a young orphan whimpered. A gentle male voice spoke quietly to him and he settled back to sleep. The room eventually quieted but sleep still eluded Sydney. She stood and wrapped the thick wool blanket around her body, then stopped for a moment to check on Jordan and found him sleeping deeply. Nearby her father and Daniel also slept the peaceful sleep of the righteous and the exhausted.

Sydney carefully picked her way through the sleeping miners and out to the foyer where she settled into a corner of the soft leather couch that faced the large front windows. Tucking her feet underneath her, she stared at the dark glass and thought about all that had happened since the day of Shannon's death. She relived, as she had a thousand times, her sister's brutal murder.

Why had her own life been spared when Shannon's had been so cruelly taken? The burden of guilt pressed on her, suffocated her, and made her unworthy of anyone's kindness or love. Would she ever be able to atone for her cowardice?

Sydney sat until the window began to pale with the first

pearly gray light of early dawn. She knew the answer. Shannon had died because of Sydney. It was the same as if she had been the one to break her sister's neck. She shivered in spite of the warm blanket.

Someone cleared their throat softly and broke into her thoughts. She turned and saw her father standing at the opposite end of the couch.

"Mind if I join you?" he whispered, then sat down without waiting for an answer.

Her father. Sydney had felt so happy to find him alive, but now every time she looked at her father he reminded her of Shannon. Her secret guilt weighed heavier and heavier with each passing day. Soon it would become unbearable and destroy her.

She had to tell him. Shannon was his daughter and he loved her. She had to suck it up and tell him.

Knowing what she had to do frightened Sydney and made it hard to breath. She cleared her throat and tried to swallow the lump that threatened to choke her.

"I need," she rasped, and stopped. She cleared her throat again.

"I need to tell you something. Something bad. Some-thing…beyond terrible."

Her father looked at her and waited. Unable to meet his eyes, Sydney focused on the tile floor.

"How bad can it be?" he asked in a quiet voice.

Tears sprung to Sydney's eyes and she forced herself to look at her father's face.

"The worst." Her breath caught on a ragged sob.

"I've told you about my twin sister Shannon," she contin-ued. "You loved her very much, you know. She was definitely a Daddy's girl. You loved me too, I know that. We both liked to camp and canoe and hike but Shannon was the one who loved to climb into your lap in the evenings when we were little and be held and read to."

She took a deep breath. She felt icy and feverish all at the same time. This was so hard to speak out loud.

"Sometimes I felt jealous of her. We competed for your and Mom's attention, but we were very close too. We were each other's best friend and we watched each other's backs. Until the day I didn't."

"Didn't what? Love your sister anymore?" Her father's voice was soft, curious.

Sydney shook her head.

"No," she whispered. "Until the day I didn't watch her back. I watched the bad men rape and kill her and I hid like the coward I am instead of helping her."

"I see." Her father got to his feet.

He was leaving. Now that he knew what a terrible person she was he couldn't bear to be near her.

She thought her heart was going to break. Again. How much pain can one woman bear? she wondered.

To Sydney's surprise, her father didn't leave. He sat down next to her. "How many bad men were there, Sydney?"

"F-four."

"And where were you?" Her father's tone sounded firm and businesslike.

"I was in Pop's barn, up in the loft. Her screams woke me from a nap. I'd been up all night looking after our grandfather. He had dementia and had come close to burning down the house the night before. I hadn't gotten much sleep because I kept watch on him for the rest of the night."

"Four grown men. Were you armed?"

Sydney shook her head. Tears ran down her face and her lips trembled.

"My bow and knife were hidden in the house. I was afraid

Pops would find them and hurt himself so I hid them in the crawl space that runs under the eaves."

Her father reached out and found her left hand. He sandwiched her hand between his own two. She almost swooned at the comforting warmth of his strong, rough hands.

"What could you have done against four men, Sydney?" he asked quietly. "If you had tried to save Shannon the men would have also raped and killed you. You had no choice in the matter. You did not hide out of cowardice, you hid out of intelligence and the desire to live. The desire to live is possibly the strongest motivator of all in any species. You did the right thing, honey."

"But-but Shannon…my poor sister. She must have been counting on me to save her and I let her down."

Her father shook his head.

"I don't agree. From what you've told me about your sister I know she was also intelligent and that she loved you. I believe she felt grateful that you stayed hidden. She would have felt terrible if you had suffered the same fate because of her. She *wanted* you to survive."

He rubbed Sydney's hand while he looked at her, his expression serious.

"Put yourself in Shannon's place—would you have wanted your sister to come to your aid, only to be raped and murdered because she tried to help you? No, I don't believe you would. You did the right thing, Sydney," he repeated.

"I miss her so much." Tears ran down Sydney's face. "She was the better of the two of us. It should've been me who died that day."

Her father stood and pulled her to her feet and wrapped his arms around her. He hugged her close, rocking her gently and stroking her hair while she cried out all her pain.

"Shannon was blessed to have you for a sister," he said

firmly. "I bet if she was standing in your place right now she'd say the same things about you, that it should have been her who died that day. Loving someone makes us vulnerable, Sydney, but it also makes us better people. Instead of carrying guilt over something you were powerless to prevent, remember the good times and the love you shared with your sister, and remember how bravely she faced her death. Be proud of her. I think you owe her that."

Sydney nodded her head. Her sobs slowly subsided. It felt good to be comforted by her father in the same way he had comforted her when she was a little girl and something hurt.

She had no idea how long her father stood and held her until she finally stepped away from him. The sun had cleared the horizon and cast bright diamond shapes through the windows onto the foyer floor.

She wiped the tears from her face.

"Thank you. Sorry I cried all over you." She looked up at her father and saw compassion and understanding and affection in his eyes.

"I know I've said this before, but if I could choose a daughter she'd be just like you, Sydney. You're smart, brave, and a very special young woman. Any man would be proud to claim you as his daughter. I'd like it very much if you would go back to calling me Daddy. Let Shannon's ghost rest. You don't have to carry her around anymore."

CHAPTER 21

JOURNEY'S END

Sydney sat beside Medicine Woman and raised her face to the sun, reveling in its warmth on her cheeks and bare shoulders. Bird song and laughter, clear and loud and joyous, filled the air. Today marked the summer solstice, the longest day of the year. In a short while Medicine Woman would officially hand her badger skin bag and pipe, the symbols of her position as healer for the village, to Sydney, and Sydney would become the village's new Medicine Woman.

She thought back to the winter solstice and the night she had almost lost her life on a snowy mountainside. She turned her head to her right and sought out her father. He beamed with pride and winked at her. She smiled back, feeling his love.

She could never repay Jordan, Dogma, Daniel, and her father for the way they had come after her and saved her from Big Mike. That wouldn't stop her from trying. There was nothing she wouldn't do for any of them.

Mallory Dunne, the deranged cult leader who had been

the cause of so much pain and death, had disappeared that same night along with some of her gold. As the temple followers blamed Mallory for the deaths of their brothers, fathers, and sons, Mallory had been wise to run rather than face the women's wrath.

The old lodge was large enough to house all of the rescued miners and the temple women. They had decided to continue with Mallory's self-sufficient community while disbanding the Temple of Gaia.

Sydney, along with Daniel, her father, and Jordan, had a standing invitation to visit the lodge whenever they were in the area. Even Dogma was welcome.

As Sydney watched, an attractive, middle-aged woman came up to her father and linked her arm through his. Sydney caught her bottom lip with her teeth and furrowed her brow. She watched the way her father looked at the woman and read the love in the woman's face.

Her father had been alone long enough. He had made a place for himself in this village of refugees and was much respected for his knowledge and ability to bring in food. Alex Waters fed the elderly and those unable to care for themselves. He was a kind and thoughtful man who deserved to find some happiness. Although she had always looked up to her father, Sydney had never felt more proud to be his daughter as she did now.

She leaned back and caught Smokey's eye. Her old friend nodded at her in his usual solemn fashion. She had been overwhelmed with happiness when Jordan had informed her that Smokey was Daniel's grandfather and Medicine Woman's son.

The reunion between Smokey and Sydney had been bittersweet. They sat together for hours and remembered the people they had loved who were now gone. Smokey had questioned her closely about her journey to find him. When Sydney finished her retelling he expressed his satisfaction at the way she had handled herself during the difficult situations she had faced.

As the village elder male, Smokey had met with Sydney the previous evening to hear any confessions she needed to make before assuming the mantle of village healer.

Thanks to her father, Sydney had come to her old friend unburdened. Instead they had passed a pleasant evening reminiscing about the summer Smokey had taken Sydney under his wing and taught her the ways of Slow Walking.

Sydney now knew that Smokey's real lesson in teaching her to slow walk was to make her aware of the earth and all its creatures. Slow walking allowed the rhythms of the earth to seep into the walker and made them as one. When a person becomes one with someone or something, they care for it and take care of it.

Smokey taught the skill to anyone willing to learn. As he had confessed to Sydney the previous evening, his goal was to teach as many humans as possible to honor and cherish their living earth home.

She reached out her left hand and placed it on Jordan's knee. He sat beside her, proud and straight as he watched the people gathered before them. Jordan's second sight enabled him to lead a useful and productive life among people who accepted his unusual ability without judgement.

The children especially loved Jordan. He had been adopted by the village as "Uncle J" and often volunteered to look after the young ones while their parents and older siblings did the work that made the village thrive.

A week ago today Jordan and Sydney had been married before the entire village with Dogma standing between them. Her father had given her away and proudly proclaimed her his daughter. Medicine Woman had performed the short ceremony, her dark eyes filled with joyous tears in her round wrinkled face as she pronounced them man and wife.

Sydney's heart had felt so full she feared it might burst open. The look of love and wonder and happiness on Jordan's face told her that he had felt the same. They had faced a long, difficult journey together and survived by trusting in one another. By learning to trust in love.

Now they faced a journey together of a different sort, one that involved raising a family, and helping others to survive the difficulties of this new world.

A quick bark caught Sydney's attention. She twisted to look behind her and saw one of the older boys holding a young girl steady on Dogma's back. The girl squealed with delight, leaned forward, and buried her beaming face in Dogma's ruff. Dogma's expression said it all—she was in doggy heaven. The great beast loved children and took on the task of child care alongside Jordan with a surprising level of patience.

It was a happy village. Every member had begun to heal from the pain of their losses. Together they were learning how to forge a new way of life.

Sydney's heart filled with love as she looked about her at the people who made up her new family and the people who would soon be her responsibility.

She felt Jordan's gaze upon her and turned her head to look into the warm gray eyes of the man who had set this all in motion. Sydney recalled the day Jordan had trapped her in his storm cellar, a desperate act that had started them down a winding path and then led them to this moment.

That day had turned out to be the luckiest day of her life.

I'm glad you found this book out of the millions available. If you'd like to know what else I've written or when I release a new book instead of leaving it to chance, you can sign up for my newsletter or send me an email through my website CharleyMarshBooks.com. I love to hear from my readers.

And if you want to know what I'm up to on a more regular basis you can follow me on Facebook. https://www.facebook.com/charley.marsh.372

ABOUT THE AUTHOR

In my younger days my curiosity drove me to climb mountains, canoe rivers, and explore caves and wilderness areas from Maine to California. I've been shot at, caught in a desert flash flood, and almost drowned off the Maine coast. Once I tobogganed down a 5,000+ foot mountain.

Life is always an adventure if you have the right attitude.

I never set out to be a storyteller, but looking back on the elaborate lies I made up as a troubled teen I can see that I always had the makings. Now, in the immortal words of Lawrence Block, I happily "make up lies for fun and profit."